SPANKING
SHAKESPEARE

A Book Sense Children's Pick
An ALA-YALSA Best Book for Young Adults
A *Publishers Weekly* Flying Start

"High-school life at its most embarrassing, hilarious best."
—*New York Post*

★ "Bold and bawdy. Wizner knows just how
to set up his outrageous jokes."
—*Publishers Weekly*, Starred

"Wizner infuses [Shakespeare's] voice with an over-the-top, biting
wit that punches his seemingly sane life episodes into knee-slapping,
lewd-icrous territory. Alternating between Shakespeare's reality
and his writing, Wizner's first novel packs the stitches tight."
—*Kirkus Reviews*

"Wizner endows his narrator with a hilarious, self-deprecating
comedic voice. Laughs alone make this effort successful, but Wizner
allows Shakespeare to grow and learn just a little, too—
an extraordinary feat for such a raucous read."
—*School Library Journal*

For Kira

17 DOWN

SENIOR YEAR

SPANKING
SHAKESPEARE

17 DOWN

WHAT'S IN A NAME?

It's hard to imagine what my parents were
thinking when they decided to name me
Shakespeare. They were probably drunk,
considering the fact that my father is an
alcoholic and my mother gets loopy after one
glass of wine. I've given up asking them
about it because neither of them is able to
remember anything anymore, and the stories
they come up with always leave me feeling
like it might not be so bad to dig a hole in
the backyard and hide out there until I
leave for college next year. That is, if I
get into college.

My mom used to tell me that she and my
father put the names of history's greatest
writers and artists and musicians into a
bowl and decided I would be named for
whoever they pulled out. "I was hoping for
van Gogh," she said.

"Didn't he cut his ear off?" I asked.

"Yes," my mother said dreamily, stroking the side of my face. "To give to the woman he loved."

My dad remembers that he and my mom always talked about giving me an "S-H" name to match the "S-H" of our last name, Shapiro. "We thought about Sherlock, Shaquille, and Shaka Zulu before we settled on Shakespeare."

"You really wanted to make my life miserable, didn't you?" I asked.

My father licked the rim of his martini glass. "That was the plan."

The worst was the time my mom came running into my room and told me she finally remembered how she and my dad had come up with my name.

"We did crazy things when we were younger," she said.

"Is this going to traumatize me?" I asked.

"Sometimes we would dress up in costumes."

"I don't want to hear this. You're an insane woman."

"We were doing a scene from Shakespeare on the day you were conceived."

"I'm calling Child Services!" I yelled, running from the room.

Her voice shrilled after me. "Your father was Othello!"

Take a moment to consider the implications of a name like Shakespeare Shapiro. It's the first day of middle school. Everybody is trying hard not to look nervous and self-conscious and miserable. I have intense pains in my stomach and begin to wonder if it's possible to get an ulcer in sixth grade.

"Good morning, everyone," the teacher says. "Please say 'here' when I call your name."

Michael and Jennifer and David and Stephanie and all the others hear their names and dutifully identify themselves.

"Shakespeare Shapiro," the teacher calls out.

The class bursts into laughter.

"Here," I squeak.

She looks up. "What a fabulous name. I've

never had a student named Shakespeare
before."

Everybody is staring at me and
whispering. If the teacher doesn't call the
next name soon, the situation will become
critical. Already I can see some of the more
ape-like boys sizing me up for an afternoon
beating.

"I bet you're a wonderful writer,
Shakespeare," she says kindly.

I begin to wish for a large brick to fall
on her head.

She looks back down at her roster.

Come on, I think. You can do it.

Her head pops back up.

"Just read the next name!" I blurt out.

And so, less than ten minutes into my
middle school career, I'm already in trouble,
and all because of my ridiculous name.

This is the story of my life, which has been
a series of catastrophes, one after another.
I'd like to say there have been some happy
times, too, but the reality is that with
seventeen years down, nothing much has gone
right so far. As I begin my senior year of

high school, here are the facts I wake up to
each morning and go to sleep with each
night:

1. After six years of elementary school,
   three years of middle school, and
   three years of high school, I have
   only two close friends: Neil
   Wasserman, whose favorite thing to do
   is discuss his bowel movements; and
   Katie Marks, whose favorite thing to
   do is tell me how pathetic I am.
2. I have never had a girlfriend,
   never kissed a girl, and spend most
   Saturday nights watching TV with my
   parents before whacking off to
   Internet porn in my bedroom.
3. My younger brother—two years
   younger—has a girlfriend, is
   extremely popular, and will
   definitely lose his virginity before
   I do.

I should warn you. Some of the material
you're about to read is disturbing. Some of
it will make you shake your head in

disbelief. Some of it will make you cringe
in disgust. Some of it might even make you
rush out into the stormy night, rip your
shirt from your body, and howl, "WHY, GOD,
WHY?"

Then again, maybe you'll just sit back
and smile, secure in the knowledge that your
name is not Shakespeare Shapiro, and this is
not your life.

SENIOR YEAR
SEPTEMBER

My high school is named after Ernest Hemingway, a writer who consumed tremendous amounts of alcohol, wrote simple declarative sentences, and eventually killed himself with a double-barreled shotgun. Hemingway High School claims to offer the finest writing program in New York. Every twelfth grader must take a year-long seminar, and it is in this class that we are expected to complete our senior project, a major piece of writing about our lives. These memoirs, often in excess of one hundred pages, have made the school famous. Not only has the award for best senior memoir eclipsed the valedictory award for graduation's most prestigious honor, but also a major publisher has offered contracts to several past winners.

To guide us through this massive undertaking, we get either Ms. Glass, who is boring, Ms. McCurry, who is mean and boring, or Mr. Parke, who is completely off his rocker. In my years at Hemingway High School, I have often seen Mr. Parke wandering the halls, smiling and nodding at the throngs of students, or else deep in conversation with himself, completely oblivious to the commotion around him. Nobody knows exactly how old he is, but I'd guess he must be at least seventy. He has thick glasses and hair sticking out of his nose and wears old blazers that have been patched at the elbows. School lore has it that in his younger days he used to drink a lot and make passes at his female students. Even now there is something faintly lecherous about him.

I am in Mr. Parke's morning class, along with the typical assortment of dumb jocks, pseudo-intellectuals, burnouts, computer geeks, freaks of nature, girls who don't know I exist, and girls who know I exist but would never go out with me. A random sampling of my classmates might include Sylvester Valentine, who caused a stir by cross-dressing for an entire week last year; Rocco Mackey, who laughs every time Mr. Parke mentions periods or colons; and Dixie Crawford, who helps boys like Rocco Mackey reproduce.

The one bright spot is Celeste Keller, who has been a star in my fantasy life since ninth grade. Celeste is moderately beautiful in that glasses-wearing, disarming-smile kind of way. She's smart and outgoing and passionate about political causes, and she reads long books by writers with Russian names, though I try not to hold that against her. I would have asked her out by now, but when you struggle with issues of self-confidence, have a mortal fear of public humiliation, and know that your hair looks puffy, these things need to be handled delicately. So I pretend not to be interested and hope for the best.

The first day of class, Mr. Parke announces he will be sharing excerpts from the memoir prologues we submitted over the summer. This is not good. In fact, it is potentially catastrophic. I suffer through one selection after another, feeling the pains in my stomach intensify and wondering if it is possible to get an ulcer in twelfth grade. I'm such a nervous wreck I barely react when Mr. Parke pauses at one point, looks up at no one in particular, and states, "I'd give my left testicle to write a sentence like that," before plunging back into the text.

Mine is last. He reads the section about my first day of middle school, then looks up with a wry smile. "Isn't it terrible," he says, "the way some teachers embarrass their students?"

At the end of class, he gives us our next assignment. We are to go home and write our obituaries.

Everybody starts asking questions all at once, but my head is already spinning with possibilities. I have spent a lot of time over the years thinking about how I might die. Usually I imagine my airplane going down or a piece of concrete from a construction job falling on my head. Sometimes I think about being buried alive, starving to death in jail, facing a firing squad, or being pushed in front of a train. But the idea of being flattened by a six-hundred-pound sumo wrestler is probably my most original concoction.

Shakespeare Shapiro, 27,

Sumo Wrestler and Haiku Poet

TOKYO, September 9 (AP)

Shakespeare Shapiro, an American-born
sumo wrestler, died here today after
being flattened by a 600-pound
opponent during an exhibition match.
Mr. Shapiro, who developed an intense
interest in sumo wrestling while
studying haiku poetry in Japan, gained
international notoriety for his
controversial use of the "nutcracker
technique," something he claimed was
necessary to stay competitive with men
more than three times his weight.

The son of an alcoholic father and
a neurotic mother, Mr. Shapiro endured
a torturous childhood, made worse by
his social ineptitude and uncanny
ability to transform any situation
into a full-blown catastrophe. After
barely surviving high school, Mr.
Shapiro worked for several months as a
crash-test dummy and sperm donor
before enrolling in a local community
college. It was in college that Mr.

Shapiro first felt a woman's breast, an event that led to six months in jail and a restraining order preventing him from coming within 50 feet of a breast-feeding mother. "It was a dark time in my life," Mr. Shapiro later wrote. "I experimented with alcohol, drugs, and cross-dressing, but nothing seemed to work. Then I discovered haiku."

In haiku, Mr. Shapiro found a poetic form that could perfectly capture what he had come to see as the essential bleakness and despair of the human condition. In one poem, he wrote: *Everything is pain / Life a cloak of suffering / I was circumcised*. His passion for haiku led to his second arrest, when he attacked a drunken man in a bar who was reciting limericks.

His fanatical desire to write the perfect haiku led him to Japan to study with the ancient haiku masters, but he became disheartened after learning that haiku does not

necessarily need to have 17 syllables.
"It was a dark time in my life," Mr.
Shapiro later wrote. "I experimented
with prostitution, competitive karaoke,
and self-mutilation. Then I discovered
sumo wrestling."

Shakespeare Shapiro competed in more
than 200 sumo wrestling matches over
five years, never winning and sustaining
multiple injuries that left him
hospitalized on numerous occasions. "He
was just a horrible wrestler," said his
brother, Gandhi. "But then again, he was
horrible at everything. Frankly, I'm
surprised he lasted as long as he did."

Mr. Shapiro is survived by his
parents, his brother, and his pet
goldfish, Sushi.

"Delightful, just delightful," Mr. Parke says as he rambles into
class with our assignments a few days later. "Some of you have
lived truly magnificent lives." He rifles through the papers. "Ah,
here we are." He begins to read Celeste's obituary, and she puts
her hands over her glasses and face—just for a moment—then
looks up with that disarming smile. Celeste's life, of course, is
extraordinary: several prestigious journalism awards, the

founding of a widely acclaimed women's literary magazine, a Pulitzer Prize, and the realization at the age of sixty-five that her fame and accomplishments have left her unfulfilled. She dies, having spent the final twelve years of her life running a school for orphans in India.

"Bravo, Ms. Keller," Mr. Parke says. "We should all be so noble." He winks at Dixie Crawford, who is staring at Rocco Mackey and fingering her low neckline.

"Galaxy Veeder," he says, pulling a second paper from the stack, "88, Astronomer." Galaxy's obituary is a clever play on her unusual name—her childhood dreams of wanting to be a star, her marriage to a former Mr. Universe, her addiction to moonshine. When Mr. Parke finishes reading, I expect him to make some crude reference to Uranus, but thankfully he just smiles and brandishes a third paper in the air.

"Mr. Mackey," he says. "Quite an interesting approach to the assignment. I'm not sure I've ever seen an obituary with such a graphic picture attached." He holds up Rocco's paper, which shows a man being shot by several heavily armed thugs, and has the caption KINGPIN ROCCO MACKEY GUNNED DOWN IN MAFIA HIT. The class laughs, and Rocco flexes his arms and kisses his biceps.

When the class has quieted, Mr. Parke pulls a fourth paper from the pile. "We have among us," he says, "someone whose remaining time is rather short." And with no further introduction, he reads my obituary, word for word, beginning to end, to the entire class. People turn to look at me as he reads, and there are nods and chuckles, and I wonder what Celeste is thinking.

I'm convinced that if I ever do get a girl to go out with me, it will be because of my writing. I had a piece published in the school literary magazine last year, a retelling of the biblical flood story that explored, among other things, masturbation, incest, bestiality, and the proper use of pronouns. Celeste told me she thought it was very funny and touched my arm while we were talking. Is it possible that my obituary will produce an even more stimulating result?

"This," Mr. Parke says when he has finished, "is the work of a writer who is not afraid to take risks with his material. Bravo, Mr. Shapiro."

After class, a few people say they liked my obituary. Sylvester Valentine thanks me for the cross-dressing reference. Rocco Mackey high-fives me and says, with what seems like genuine admiration, that I have a sick mind. And Mr. Parke pulls me aside and says he hopes to see more of the same as the semester progresses.

Celeste is waiting for me by the door. She is wearing jeans and a black sweater, and her brown curls fall loosely to her shoulders. She smells like tangerines.

"I liked your obituary," she says with a smile that makes me tingle.

"Thanks. I liked yours, too." I can feel my hair puffing up and wonder whether I can pat it down without her noticing.

We walk out of the room in silence, and a million thoughts race through my mind. Say something witty. Ask her something about herself. Compliment her on her writing. Offer up an amusing anecdote. Don't stare at her chest.

"What class do you have now?" I ask.

"French. Or should I say *'Français'*?" As the word rolls off her lips, she tilts her head and holds her hand to her breast. "That's how Madame Broussard talks," she says with a little laugh.

"I hear she's crazy."

Celeste nods. "She's certainly passionate. I call her Madame Ovary."

We come to the end of the hallway. "My class is upstairs," she says, taking off her glasses and polishing them on her sweater.

I suddenly become convinced my fly is unzipped, and I move my arm in front of my crotch as inconspicuously as possible.

She flashes that smile. "See you later, I guess."

I watch her begin up the stairs. *"Adiós,"* I call after her. "I mean, *au revoir.*" Idiot.

Ten minutes later Ms. Rigby, my math teacher, calls on me when I'm not paying attention. Ms. Rigby is the kind of teacher who prowls for students not paying attention and pounces on them with undisguised delight. I've been staring at Jody Simons, who is wearing a miniskirt and sitting diagonally in front of me, and when Ms. Rigby calls my name, my head shoots up and my cheeks begin to burn.

"Shakespeare," she says. "If you would devote as much focus to calculus as you do to Jody's legs, you might learn some math this year."

Everybody laughs, and Jody shoots me a sympathetic look, the kind you might offer to the parent of a brain-dead child.

In the hallway after class, I see my younger brother walking hand in hand with his girlfriend. Don't look, I tell myself, you don't need to see this. But it's never easy to turn away from scenes of carnage and mutilation. I hurry to the cafeteria, get some food, and find Neil and Katie at our usual corner table.

"What's up, loser?" Katie says as I sit down. She's wearing her army jacket even though it's probably eighty degrees in the cafeteria.

Neil surveys my tray. "I was just telling Katie about the gigantic crap I took last time I ate these school enchiladas. Remember that?"

Katie groans. "Are we going to spend this whole lunch talking about your bowel movements?"

Neil takes a bite of his enchilada. "Why, do you have something more interesting to discuss?"

"Anything's more interesting," she says. "Come on, Shakespeare, tell us what horrible things happened to you this morning."

Sometimes I think Katie only hangs out with us because she likes being around people who are even more miserable than she is. Also, we're probably the only people who would put up with her constant stream of cynicism and abuse.

I look around to make sure no one from my math class is nearby; then I tell them about getting caught staring at Jody's legs.

"Pervert," Katie says.

I take a sip of milk. "Plus I made an idiot of myself in front of Celeste."

"Celeste again?" Neil says through chewed-up cheese and beans.

Katie gives me a disgusted look. "Jesus, Shakespeare! You just need to screw this girl already."

"Why don't you ask her out?" Neil says, studying his enchilada and trying to figure out if he can stuff the rest of it in his mouth without it falling apart. "You've been talking about her since ninth grade."

"These things can't be rushed," I say.

"Jesus!" Katie blurts out. "If there was anyone in this goddamn place that I didn't think was a total asshole, I would have screwed him five hundred times by now."

Neil looks up. "I'm available."

"Don't make me puke." Katie stands and picks up her tray. "I'll see you losers later."

"Hey," Neil says. "If you're not gonna finish your food, I'll eat it."

Katie takes her plate off her tray and hands it to him. "You're sick," she says.

He attacks the half-eaten enchilada with quick, jerky movements, looking more like a woodpecker than a human being. Neil's nose actually is rather beak-like, but it fits his tall, lanky frame. Much more jarring, at least to me, is how someone who eats like a hippopotamus could be a poster child for famine relief.

"So," Neil says, "what are you going to do about Celeste?"

I watch a pair of junior girls walk past and make a quick calculation of which one I'd rather sleep with. "Listen, Neil," I say. "When you've been burned as many times as I have, you learn to proceed with extreme caution."

"What are you talking about? You've never even asked a girl out."

I nod. "Exactly."

"So how do you know what will happen if you don't even try?"

I take a bite of my enchilada. "She used to go out with Jordan Miller. Why would she want to go out with someone like me?"

Neil opens his mouth to speak, then catches himself. "Well," he says at last, "Jordan's away at college now."

"Harvard."

"So what? He's not here. Celeste's single."

We could go on like this for hours, but suddenly the futility and frustration of it all sweeps over me. "Okay, Neil, it's really simple. Yes, I could ask Celeste out, and maybe, possibly, she might say yes. But here's what would probably happen. She would get really uncomfortable because she'd quickly realize how lame I am. She wouldn't want to make me feel bad, so she would say something like 'I don't want to do anything that could ruin our friendship,' and even though we're not really friends, I would play along and tell her I understand, and then I would have to spend the rest of the year trying to avoid her, which would be impossible since we have a class together, and any illusion I might be holding on to that she secretly likes me would be completely and irrevocably shattered."

Neil considers this for a moment. "So are you going to ask her out?"

"I'll think about it," I say.

I do think about it. I think about it every day as I sit next to Celeste in class. I think about it every night as I lie in bed committing mass spermicide. It shouldn't be so hard, I tell myself. Guys ask girls out all the time. Every day that I hesitate, hundreds of thousands of high school boys are busy having sex. But how do you actually get there? What do you actually say? Hi, Celeste, I really like you. Would you like to go out sometime? Hi, Celeste, I've been finding myself thinking about you all the time. Maybe you'd like to go see a movie after school? Hi, Celeste, I really want to get laid this year, and right now you're the most likely candidate.

I wonder how Gandhi did it. He's going out with this girl Meredith, who's actually pretty cute. He never talked about it with me. He never acted like he had a crush on a girl. One day last year I saw them holding hands in the hallway, and when I asked him about it that night, he said she was someone he had just started going out with.

But how? I wanted to ask. What did you say? What did she say back? Of course when you're sixteen and your brother is fourteen, you can't really ask him to teach you how to get a girlfriend. Sometimes I wish we were still in elementary school so I could beat him up like I used to.

Mr. Parke says that writing our memoirs will help us understand ourselves better. He says that exploring our pasts will help us uncover the themes of our lives. What has become evident to me is that the course of my life was set very early. From the beginning, the Fates were conspiring against me.

THE EARLY YEARS

I was born on Hitler's birthday. Whenever I did anything wrong as a child, my father would call me Adolf, and my mother, whose parents had been Holocaust survivors, would fly into a fury and accuse my father of being an insensitive pig. They would scream and shout at each other, fingers pointed and spittle flying, until one of them would remember that I was in the room. Not that it mattered. I always had unusually large accumulations of wax in my ears, so I rarely heard anything they said.

My brother, Gandhi, arrived when I was nineteen months old. He was an exceedingly violent child, who would celebrate his second birthday by kicking me in the eye and sending me to the hospital, bloodied, to be stitched up. By that time, I had already amassed an impressive collection of battle scars, including two dog bites, three bee stings, and a partially botched circumcision.

My brother and I were difficult children, but much of this was due to my parents' complete ineptitude. My father liked to sneak up behind us, make a scary face, and scream, "I'm going to eat you!" We would cry in terror as my father became himself again, gently comforting us and making funny faces and sounds until we started to laugh. Then, just as we had calmed down, he would spring his monster face on us again, sending us into another fit of howling and screaming.

My mother played games of a different sort. When she had had enough of our screaming and fighting, she would pretend we did not exist. We could call for her or tug on her leg, but nothing would get her to notice us. "I wonder where the kids are?" she would say as we sobbed hysterically. "I hope they're not dead."

We hated to go to sleep at night, so my father would bribe us with new installments of Nebuchadnezzar Schwartz, a running story he had created about an evil king with a penchant for torturing children. Each night, tucked beneath my blankets, I would listen to tales of disobedient children forced to kiss giant cockroaches, eat dead rats, or lick dirty toilet seats in large commuter railway stations. "Now go to sleep," my father would say when he had finished, "because Nebuchadnezzar Schwartz saves his worst punishments for children who don't go to bed when they're told."

On the nights when my parents threw parties, my brother and I refused to stay in bed, so my parents used us as props to entertain the guests. By the time I was three, they had taught me a few routines, and I was expected to perform these on demand. As people milled around with their drinks, my dad would whisper in my ear and hand me a glass of apple juice and a spoon. I would climb on a chair, bang the spoon on my glass, and when everybody was quiet, hold up my glass and say, "I'd like to make a toast." Sometimes I got it wrong and said, "I'd like to have some toast," but this would make the guests laugh even harder. On other occasions, I would greet guests at the door and say, "You must be here for the funeral." I never understood why these routines were funny and much preferred to create my own. These included running around the apartment making farting noises, waging fake gun battles with my brother, and dumping whatever I could find onto the floor.

We were wild boys, and my parents could not contain us. Anything that was standing, we would do our best to topple. Anything that could be broken, we would do our best to break. My parents put locks on the refrigerator, locks on the cabinets, locks on the telephones, and still it was not enough. My mother took us to the doctor to see if there was something wrong with us. "They fight all the time," she said. "They run around the apartment like wild animals."

"You were an only child, weren't you?" the doctor asked.

My mother nodded.

"They're fine," the doctor said. "That's the way little boys act."

But apparently I was not fine. When I was four, my parents decided I needed to see a therapist because I had stopped using the toilet. I had been trained a year earlier but had suddenly begun walking into closets and crapping in my pants. There were other issues, I think—a perverse fascination with ketchup, a habit of humping my younger brother—but the toilet problem seemed to upset my parents the most.

My therapist's name was Celia, and after she met with me, she told my parents that I needed to come every day. "There's a lot of pent-up anger," she said. "This will take some time."

I enjoyed my afternoon sessions with Celia. We would draw pictures together and play with toys, and she always seemed very interested in everything I did.

"Do you like crashing trucks together?" she would ask as I played with the cars on her floor.

Or she would look at my drawings and ask, "Is that a picture of you and your brother? Why are you standing on his face?"

I remember that Celia had a little dog who used to climb on my lap and lick me all over. I loved the dog and would laugh and shriek as we played together. One day the dog became so excited that she urinated all over me, and for the next several weeks my toilet issues reached unspeakable levels of perversity. I never saw that little dog again.

At about the time I started kindergarten, Celia told my parents that I had made substantial progress and they should see how I did without therapy for a while. With my toilet issues resolved, I entered kindergarten poised for success.

The first day, we sat in a big circle on the rug and played games to get to know each other. The teacher put us in pairs and we had to introduce our new special friends to the class. My partner was a boy named Udi who had recently arrived from Israel and spoke only a few words of English. His accent, the wax in my ears, and my own predisposition to bowel movements all conspired against me, and when I introduced him, I said, "This is Doody."

All the kids started to laugh, and I realized how funny it sounded. "This is Doody!" I screamed.

The teacher grew very red and shouted for quiet. Then she fixed me with a stern look and said, "Shakespeare, go sit in the corner. We do not make fun of other people's names. How would you like it if people teased you because of your name?"

I don't remember exactly what went through my mind as I sat in a little chair in the corner staring at the wall, but I feel certain that some of my earliest ideas about the lack of fairness and justice in the world were beginning to take shape. Before the year was out, these ideas would be dramatically reinforced.

Sally Hill was the most precocious five-year-old in my kindergarten class. She had been reading books since age three, could spell words like *elephant* and *bumblebee*, ate sushi with chopsticks at lunch, and, most astounding, had begun to experiment with sarcasm. If someone said something stupid, she would say, "That's so brilliant." If someone brought an orange peel or a scribbled-on piece of construction paper for show-and-tell, she would nod her head and say, "I wish I had one of those." Most of the kids thought she was being nice, but I knew better.

Sally and I had known each other all our

lives. Our families lived close to each
other, and our parents were friends. We
had spent time at each other's houses,
played together, and watched each other
grow into the five-year-olds we had become.
I loved spending time with Sally because
she always came up with ideas that were
much more imaginative than anything I could
come up with on my own. I suppose she
enjoyed spending time with me because she
could set all the rules, devise all the
games, and use me or discard me as she saw
fit.

Most of Sally's games involved elaborate
role-playing. Her favorite was one in which
she played a teacher and I played a student
who could never do anything right. (When I
asked her how to play my part, she said to
act like I did at school.) Sally was very
strict. Each time we played, she would yell
at me and tell me I would not get any snack
that day. Sometimes she would make me sit in
the corner facing the wall. When I told her
I didn't want to play anymore, she would
tell me that I had been very good and give
me a sticker, and I would allow myself to be

sucked into another round of verbal and emotional abuse.

One day Sally said she had a new game she wanted to play. The rules were simple. I would pull down my pants and show her mine, and then she would pull down her pants and show me hers. Even at age five, I knew exactly what she was talking about, and I also knew it was something we were not supposed to do. At the same time, I was curious to see what she had and what it looked like and to ask her how it worked. I stood there frozen, not sure what to do or say.

"Come on," she said impatiently. "We don't have much time." Obviously she knew we were doing something wrong, too, and while this might have been a major turn-on in later years, it was horribly unsettling to my five-year-old self.

"I don't think we should," I said nervously.

I had always done whatever Sally told me to do, so this refusal, however weak, was new to both of us. We stood there in my bedroom looking at each other.

"We'll do it at the same time," she finally said. "Ready, set, go." And just like that I found myself unbuttoning my pants, unzipping my zipper, pulling down my pants, and pulling down my underwear. The whole thing should have lasted fewer than ten seconds, and for Sally it did. Before I could get a good look at whatever she had, she was already back in her clothes, acting as if nothing had happened. Unfortunately, as I tried to pull my underwear back up, I lost my balance and fell. I struggled to stand and dress myself at the same time, lost my balance again, crashed into my dresser, and ended up in a tangle with my penis exposed.

Sally took a good long look as I lay there helpless, and her face screwed itself up in genuine disgust. "I'm leaving," she announced.

"Wait!" I screamed. Somehow, the thought of being abandoned like this was more than I could bear, and I started to cry. I cried because what should have been a momentous event had not been momentous at all. I cried because I had barely seen hers, but she had most certainly seen mine, and what she had seen had obviously fallen short of her expectations. I cried because I felt no wiser or more experienced than I had felt before, because I had done something that I knew was dirty and wrong, and because somehow I knew that my relationship with Sally would never be the same again.

It could have been worse. No parents walked in, and nobody ever found out. But Sally had clearly lost interest in me. From that day forth, she chose her books over our games, and she paid me little attention in our hours together at school.

Twelve years have passed since that first humiliation, and Sally and I still go to school together. We are not friends, though we do say hi when we pass in the halls. She's a lesbian now, and sometimes I wonder if I am partially responsible.

OCTOBER

Senior year is about two things: getting into college and getting laid. At my school, pretty much everybody is successful at the first, but only about half the guys in any given year are successful at the second. I've come up with a few theories about why this is so.

Money. We pay tens of thousands of dollars a year to attend college, but we hope to have sex for the price of dinner and a movie.

Support. When it comes to getting into college, everybody is in your corner. You've got a guidance counselor, you've got an SAT tutor, you've got people to help you with your essay. Who do you have helping you get laid?

False Advertising. Colleges only see you on paper before they accept you, and people always look better on paper than in person. Think about it. How many people respond to personal ads thinking they've found the man or woman of their dreams, only to be bitterly disappointed when the face-to-face meeting takes place?

Safety Schools. You don't just apply to a few colleges and hope for the best. You apply to a lot of schools, including ones that are not your top choices but that you feel confident will accept you. If the object is going to college, then any school is better than no school at all. That's the secret. Just get in some-where.

You know how people make lists of all the colleges they're applying to? I decided to do the same thing with girls. Here's what I have right now:

UNREALISTIC, BUT WORTH FANTASIZING ABOUT
Jody Simons:
   Jody Simons is in the popular crowd
and has dated the boys that the
popular girls date, but something
about her seems different. For one
thing, she volunteers for the school's
community service program and tutors
disadvantaged children. For another
thing, she has friends outside the
party-going, trendsetting, partner-
swapping circle she's associated with.
And for a third thing, she told me
once she thought I had the coolest
name. Even though we've never had a
real conversation, I've convinced

myself she has a secret crush on me
that she's been nursing since we were
in a class together in tenth grade. I
could stare at her legs forever.

Lisa Kravitz:

Lisa Kravitz and I were friends in
elementary school, when she was still
awkward and flat-chested. Toward the
end of sixth grade, she blossomed into
the hottest girl in the class, and
since then I've had a huge crush on
her. She's one of those girls who's
friendly to everybody and probably
knows everyone in our grade. When she
spots me by the lockers or in the
hallway, she always seems genuinely
pleased to see me, and for a moment I
can pretend that we're still really
close. She's had a few not-so-great
boyfriends over the years. What she
needs is a nice, sensitive guy like me.

MORE REALISTIC

Celeste Keller:

The day Celeste heard my obituary
was the day our relationship took on

new life. We sit together in class now, and I smile when she makes references to novels I haven't read and wonder if this is how literary people flirt. I missed a great opportunity the other day. She was talking about a battle scene in *The Iliad* as an example of Homer-erotica, and it wasn't until later that I realized *Homer* rhymes with *boner*.

Katie Marks:

If you look closely enough at Katie, you can see that she has a pretty face and a nice body, even though she plays down her femininity as much as possible. Sometimes I fantasize about her ripping open her oversized army coat and being completely naked underneath. The way she curses, you know there would be a lot of dirty talk. The way she drinks, you know she would be wild and uninhibited. Neil says he is going to try to sleep with her, and I tell him

it's lame to talk that way about your
closest female friend.

SAFETIES
Jane Blumeberg:
   Jane Blumeberg is a sweet, shy girl
a year behind me in school. I am sure
she has never had a boyfriend or even
kissed a boy. Our families know each
other and belong to the same temple.
She always smiles when she sees me,
and I've caught her staring at me when
she didn't think I was looking. She is
actually pretty cute, with long brown
hair and big doe-like eyes, but I
think what she would like is a nice,
safe boy to hold hands with. You see
the problem.

Most any ninth-grade girl with low
self-esteem:
   I'm just kidding. Sort of.

My list of colleges is far more extensive, with at least half a
dozen schools I have absolutely no chance of getting into.
   "You never know," my mother says. "It doesn't hurt to try."

We're in the living room before dinner, and my father has just finished his second martini.

"George Bush got into Yale," he says, looking wistfully at his empty glass.

"And you're certainly smarter than he is," my mother adds.

Given that she's a high school guidance counselor, it is remarkable how little my mother understands about how colleges choose their students. Thank goodness she works at a school other than mine.

"Who wouldn't want you?" my mother says, giving me a hug.

Every girl in my high school class, for starters, I think.

"You're certainly a better writer than most of the students in my freshman seminar," my father says.

This is small consolation. My father is probably the only tenured English professor in the country who volunteers to teach a remedial writing course to incoming freshmen, and most of his students speak English as a second language. His dissertation was entitled *Chewing GUM: Sinking Our Teeth into Grammar, Usage, and Mechanics,* and I've caught him more than once salivating over a well-placed semicolon.

"Well, hopefully I'll get in somewhere," I say, because I can't resist the opportunity to provoke him.

Sure enough, his face goes red. "*Hopefully* is an adverb. Do not use it to mean 'I hope.'"

And now the farmer example.

"The farmer looked up at the sky hopefully," my father says.

I smile.

"You scoundrel," he says, and goes off to fix himself another drink.

Mr. Parke often begins class with a free-write. When we come in, he has us take out a piece of paper and make a list of the things we are most preoccupied with.

"Don't spend a lot of time thinking," he says. "Just write down whatever is on your mind."

To demonstrate, he quickly scribbles his own list on the board:

BEAUTIFUL WRITING, BEAUTIFUL WOMEN, 100-YEAR-OLD GRAND MARNIER, ALIMONY PAYMENTS, MARQUIS DE SADE.

He points to the last item. "That's the name of my Saint Bernard," he says by way of explanation, "though the original's not bad either."

"Are we going to have to share this with the class?" Eugene Gruber asks. Eugene is president of the Dungeons & Dragons club, which puts him just slightly below me on the social food chain.

"This is just for you, Eugene," Mr. Parke replies. "So don't hold back on any of those secret perversions."

The class laughs, and I join in, grateful that I am not the one they are laughing at.

On my paper I write: CELESTE, GETTING LAID, GETTING INTO COLLEGE, SATs, MEMOIR AWARD, PUBLIC HUMILIATION, MR. PARKE'S LEFT TESTICLE.

"Now," says Mr. Parke, "write for twenty minutes off the list you came up with and see where it takes you."

Eugene's hand shoots up.

"No, Eugene, you will not have to share, though I hope some people will volunteer."

I begin to write and, uncensored, the words come easily.

Stanley Kaplan and The Princeton Review Offer SEX Preparation Classes

After years of success offering SAT and other test-preparation courses, Stanley Kaplan and The Princeton Review have decided to expand their tutoring empires to prepare male teenagers for the new SEXs.

SEX, which stands for *Sex Ex*am, comes at a time when an increasing number of teenage boys are finding they lack the necessary skills to get laid. "Something had to be done," said

Hugh Hefner, founder of *Playboy*
magazine and a strong supporter of the
new testing program. "We've got a
whole generation of young men growing
up without the tools they need to be
sexually productive members of our
society."

The Sex Exam consists of two
sections. The first—Getting Someone to
Go to Bed with You—focuses on
strategies that will make you more
desirable. The second—Sexual
Performance—focuses on maximizing both
your and your partner's pleasure
during the act itself.

Testing was scheduled to begin last
year, but protests of sexual bias from
the gay community convinced test
makers and education officials that
new tests needed to be developed.
"We're very conscious of political
correctness," said an education
spokesman. "Students now have the
option of taking a version of the exam
that focuses specifically on gay sex."

Although the test is new,

representatives from Stanley Kaplan and
The Princeton Review are confident
they can prepare anybody who takes
their classes. "We'll be teaching our
courses in a revolutionary way," said
a spokesman for Stanley Kaplan. "Not
only will students work their way
through practice problems in our
review books, they will also observe
and discuss live simulations. We're
very excited about our program. I've
got a hard-on just thinking about it."

"Any volunteers to share?" Mr. Parke asks.

Rocco raises his hand.

"Mr. Mackey," Mr. Parke says with a smile. "Have you actually written something today, or are we to be treated to one of your fabulous drawings?"

"Both," Rocco says proudly.

Rocco reads a few sentences about how much he loves football. Then he holds up his drawing, which shows a huge player in a uniform that says MACKEY crashing down on a cowering quarterback.

Mr. Parke shakes his head. "Painful," he says. "On so many levels." Then, more brightly, "Any other volunteers?"

Everybody looks at everybody else.

"Share yours, Shakespeare," Rocco calls across the room. "I bet that's some funny shit."

I try to make myself as small as possible. "That's okay."

"Come on, Shakespeare," Celeste whispers. "I'm sure it's great."

Everyone is suddenly looking at me, and even Mr. Parke seems to be nodding encouragement. A few more seconds and I will lose control of the situation completely.

"It's not appropriate," I say.

Mr. Parke's eyes light up. "I should hope not."

I look down at my paper. There is no way I can read this out loud to the class. Every girl in here will think I'm some kind of pervert.

"Would you like me to read it for you?" Mr. Parke asks.

It feels like I have no choice, so I hand him my paper.

I keep my head down as he reads, and my skin prickles with excitement and anguish. Even though I go to great lengths to make myself invisible, deep down I crave the spotlight. I hear people laughing, but somehow it all seems very far away. I peek up and see Celeste looking at me and smiling.

"You're the man!" Rocco yells when Mr. Parke has finished.

Mr. Parke shakes his head. "I must say, Mr. Shapiro, your writing certainly is provocative." He hands me my paper and smiles. "Brilliant work."

Celeste comes up beside me as I leave class and puts her arm through mine. "You're bad," she says.

There are very few things more exciting than being called bad by a girl you want to do bad things to. Why, then, do I feel like I might throw up?

"Where do you come up with your ideas?" she asks.

I shrug. It's hard to concentrate with Celeste touching me.

"I get it," she says. "Great writers never reveal their inspiration."

"No, it's just . . . I don't know . . . I wish there really was a class like that," I say. "I sure could use it right now."

Celeste laughs but does not say anything.

"Do you want to maybe go to a movie after school?" I ask without looking at her.

Celeste stops and turns to me. "Today?" She has a troubled look on her face. "I can't today. I have an appointment."

"That's okay," I say quickly. "I should be working on my memoir anyway." Idiot, idiot, idiot, what were you thinking?

"I could go on Thursday," she says.

"Thursday? Yeah, Thursday's good. Great."

We stand there looking at each other, smiling awkwardly.

"So I guess I'll see you later," I say, already moving away. Miraculously, I manage to escape without tripping or bumping into any large objects.

I'm sitting in Ms. Rigby's math class basking in the glow of my conquest when the assistant principal comes in and calls Charlotte White out of class. Charlotte is a quiet, serious student, so it seems unlikely that she is in trouble. All I can think is that there must be some sort of family emergency, and when Charlotte walks from the room—quick and pale—I flash back to a poem she wrote in English last year. She never shared her work in class, but one time we were paired together, and I had to read what she had written. I remember she seemed uncomfortable sharing, and though I don't recall exactly what the poem was about, I do remember a frightening image of a girl walking across a frozen lake, and knowing somehow she was writing about herself.

She's a strange girl, Charlotte, though it's hard to pinpoint what exactly is off. It's not her clothes or her mannerisms or the way she talks. She doesn't have any tattoos or weird piercings or purple hair or unshaved legs. She's actually very plain-looking, a little tall maybe, with a slightly tomboyish face. What sets her apart, I think, is the way she always keeps to herself. It's like there's an invisible wall she's put up to keep people from getting too close. She came to the school partway through eleventh grade last year and, as far as I can tell, has never made any friends.

I push Charlotte out of my mind and return to more pleasant musings. I imagine walking through the hallways hand in hand with Celeste, and people who have never paid me any attention suddenly taking notice. I imagine acknowledging my brother and his girlfriend with a knowing grin as I wrap my arm around Celeste's shoulders. I imagine kissing Celeste by the lockers the way I've seen other couples kiss as if it's no big deal.

When I sit down at lunch I must look as smug as I feel because Katie asks me if I've just gotten laid.

"Not yet," I say with a smile.

"What happened?" Neil asks.

I draw out the silence, savoring the moment. "Got a date with Celeste on Thursday."

Neil nearly jumps out of his seat. "What happened?"

"Jesus," Katie says, looking at him. "What the hell's the matter with you?"

I tell them what happened, leaving out any moments of personal awkwardness and insecurity.

"Screw the movie," Katie says when I've finished. "Just get her drunk."

"Yeah, right," I say. "Very romantic."

"Take her to the new Showcase Cinemas," Neil says. "They have the best bathrooms."

Katie glares at him. "Could you be any more fucking pathetic?"

Neil blows her a kiss. "I love it when you talk dirty to me."

Thursday comes, and I spend most of the day making a mental list of everything that could go wrong on our date. I have little hope that things will run completely smoothly, but I am determined to avoid any large-scale catastrophes. Once we make it to the movie, I figure I will be in the clear. I mean, how much can go wrong once the movie starts?

We have planned to see a new comedy, but when we meet after school, Celeste asks if I'd rather see a South American documentary playing at the art theater downtown. "It's about the resurgence of Native American cultures in the Americas," she says. "It's supposed to be really good."

It's a documentary. It's probably going to be one of the most insufferably boring movies I have ever seen. "Sounds good," I say.

"Have you seen any of Alejandero's other films?"

Alejandero? Is that his first name or his last name? "I don't think so," I say.

"He's amazing. I saw a film he made about the domestic rituals of female Inuits that was so eye-opening."

Female Inuits. Sounds fascinating. Can I have a large shovel or a long piece of rope?

We get on the bus, and I use the opportunity to change the subject.

"How's your memoir coming along?" I ask.

Celeste takes a deep breath as if she's about to deliver some pronouncement of great consequence. "It's a challenge," she says. "I mean, you read Dostoyevsky and Tolstoy, and anything you write seems so childish and inept." She looks at me expectantly.

Just get to the theater, I think. Dark room, no more talking. "I try to stay away from writers with long Russian names."

Celeste laughs. She thinks I'm kidding.

When we get to the theater, Celeste refuses my offer to buy her ticket. "You can buy the popcorn," she says. "I'll go get seats."

I don't want popcorn. The butter makes me sick.

"And ask them to put extra butter on it," she calls back to me.

The theater is half empty, but Celeste has managed to find us seats in the middle of a nearly full row, and I have to navigate my way over the legs and past the knees of several stone-faced senior citizens who sit rigidly, refusing to make room for me to pass. This is fun, I think as I stumble over a cane. I should go on dates more often.

The buttered popcorn and my frazzled nerves conspire against me, and just as the movie starts I develop intense stomach cramps. I look down the row. The old people have formed a blockade. On the screen there is tribal chanting, and a voice-over says, "After years of oppression, now the time has come for Montezuma's revenge."

"How long is this movie?" I whisper.

"About two and a half hours."

I close my eyes. Wonderful. I'd say I've got about seven minutes before I start to crap all over this seat.

I actually hold out for twenty before I make a mad dash to

the bathroom, where I release a cacophony of sounds that would leave even Neil wide-eyed with disbelief. I don't want to go back. I don't want to step over those surly senior citizens again and then realize that my stomach is still acting up. I don't want to sit through two more hours of a movie without any plot, action, or nudity. But how long can I stay here before Celeste starts to worry and comes looking for me?

Fifteen minutes later I finally make my way back. "Are you okay?" she whispers as I slide into my seat.

I nod, though my shin is stinging from a well-placed kick from Mr. or Mrs. Medicare down the row.

Celeste remains focused on the screen. "I'll tell you what you missed when it's over."

Better yet, just shoot me now.

When the movie ends, we stand outside the theater, and I tell Celeste how interesting I thought the film was, and she tells me that I should really try to rent the Inuit film, and I tell her that I will, though it's more likely that I'll chop off my left pinkie and sell it on eBay.

Celeste looks at her watch. "I should go. I'm meeting a friend for dinner."

I nod, simultaneously relieved to be escaping our date without further damage and terrified that she is ditching me to go have dinner with some other guy. "Yeah, I need to get going myself. Are you taking the bus?"

"No, it's close." She squeezes my hand. "I'll see you tomorrow in class." Then she turns and walks off.

Bye. Feel free to discuss my bowel movements if you run out of things to talk about.

"Well, I'm glad to see the old pathetic Shakespeare is back," Katie says to me at lunch the next day.

"I hate those bathrooms," Neil says. "I told you to go to Showcase Cinemas."

I push the food around my plate.

"Oh, cheer up," Katie says. "She's a stuck-up bitch anyway."

"You think everyone is a stuck-up bitch," I say.

"Not them," she says, motioning to a table across the cafeteria where Rocco Mackey and a group of his friends are sliding their hot dogs in and out of their mouths.

"Gross," Neil says. He wipes ketchup from his tray with his finger and licks it off.

Katie smiles. "*You're* saying 'gross'? You keep a journal of your bowel movements."

Neil blushes and shoots me an angry look.

I shrug. "I didn't know it was a secret. You seem so proud of it."

"You have got to be the biggest freak I have ever met," Katie says.

"What? What's so weird about it?" Neil asks.

They begin going back and forth, and I let my eyes wander around the cafeteria. It's all so familiar, the same groups sitting in the same places having the same conversations. At one table, I notice, Charlotte White is sitting alone, hunched over a notebook, writing furiously. She is completely absorbed, writing in an uninterrupted stream, pausing only long enough to turn the page before her pen races onward. With her free hand she sweeps some strands of hair out of her face like she is shooing away a fly. What could she be writing? What kind of dark, brooding voices are lurking inside her head?

"I'll see you guys later," I say, standing and pushing away from the table. "I've got some work to do."

"Bye," Neil says without looking up. He has pulled out his special notebook and is showing a speechless Katie his "daily log."

I don't know what I'm doing, but I find myself taking a circuitous route so I can walk past Charlotte's table. As I get there, I pause, and in that moment she looks up at me and quickly closes her notebook.

I offer an embarrassed smile. "Are you working on your memoir?" I ask.

She shifts uncomfortably. "No. I mean, maybe. I mean, I don't know if I'll use any of this."

I nod, because this makes perfect sense. "Who do you have for writing seminar?"

"Mr. Parke." She puts her notebook in her bag.

"Really? Me too. What do you think of him?"

"I'm not sure," she says. Then, after a moment, "He talks about his testicles a lot."

I laugh. "Usually just the left one." It occurs to me that this is probably the longest conversation I have ever had with Charlotte White. For all I know, it's the longest conversation anyone has ever had with Charlotte White.

"I actually have to go," she says. "I'm way behind on my memoir and the quarter ends next week."

She gets up, and as she begins to walk away, I ask her what she was writing about.

She shakes her head. "It's kind of personal."

Of course it's personal. Otherwise I wouldn't be so curious. "Sorry," I say.

"Maybe if I knew you better . . ."

I tell her I understand.

She starts to walk away and then turns back. "How's your memoir going?"

"Pretty good. I'm up to the part where my parents sent me away to a camp straight out of *Lord of the Flies*."

She smiles and walks off.

Mr. Parke says memoir is not just about the events in our lives, but also what those events reveal about who we are. He says that every story we tell should have an under-story, and everything we write should serve to illuminate the themes in our lives. When I started on this chapter of my memoir, he asked me to think about what it was really about. Is it my parents' inexplicably poor judgment? Is it my unexpected and ultimately humiliating sexual awakening? Is it my earliest memories of my own insignificance?

I was six years old when my parents first sent me to camp, and the themes of my life were beginning to come into sharper focus.

THE TIME MY PARENTS SENT ME TO A CAMP STRAIGHT OUT OF *LORD OF THE FLIES*

I have no idea how my parents selected Camp Greenwood for my inaugural camp experience, but it is hard to imagine they had any prior knowledge of the workings of that horrible place.

At Camp Greenwood everyone had a military rank, and, predictably enough, distinctions were based on age. First graders were privates, second graders corporals, third graders sergeants, and so on up the ladder to eighth-grade generals. Although not officially stated in camp literature, it was understood that the higher your rank, the more power you had, and so life was not good for those of us at the bottom of the totem pole.

Every afternoon the counselors would gather the whole camp together to gamble.

The way it worked was this: the counselors
would divide themselves into two teams and
compete against each other in some sport.
The campers had to bet on which team would
win. We would signal our choices by sitting
in one of the two designated spectator
areas. If we were lucky enough to choose the
winning team, we would form a long line, by
rank, and receive candy. If we were on the
losing side, we would be summarily dismissed
to get ready for the next activity. The
biggest problem with the system—aside from
the fact that the counselors, not the kids,
were playing; aside from the fact that some
kids were getting candy and others were
getting nothing; aside from the fact that
kids were betting on adults—was the fact
that no matter who won or who lost, the
older kids always ended up with the candy
anyway. It was called the tribute system,
and it ensured that high-ranking officials
on the losing side would not feel resentment
toward low-ranking officials on the winning
side and end up inflicting some form of
corporal punishment.

The bathrooms, I quickly learned, were

places to avoid at all costs. Older boys routinely peed in the sinks, overstuffed the toilets, and drew disturbing pictures on the walls. On one occasion, before I understood how things worked at Camp Greenwood, I sat down in a stall only to be plunged into pitch-darkness as a group of boys turned off the lights and ran away laughing. Too frightened to move, too frightened to scream, I sat there for what seemed like an eternity until my counselor realized I was missing and came looking for me. "Got caught with your pants down," he said, laughing. "You'll learn."

And I did learn. I learned that the lake and the pool were the best places in the camp to urinate, and I came to savor the moment each day when I could just let myself go and feel the warmth of my urine spread around me. I never thought about the fact that many of my fellow campers were probably doing the same thing, but it would explain why the counselors never went in the water themselves and why they often referred to the pool as the toilet bowl.

It was in the camp swimming pool that I

made a truly remarkable discovery. I was standing in the water with my stomach pressed up against the side when I began to feel a tingling sensation. I adjusted myself a little and the feeling became more intense. Ten more minutes of experimentation, and I hit on something that made me gasp and push away from the wall.

So began my first love affair, and as the summer wound down, all the indignities and injustices of camp life faded away, and I lived each day in feverish anticipation of my time in the pool.

I was too young to be self-conscious, and I was too enraptured to be discreet. One day I actually yelped in pleasure, and a group of older boys stopped what they were doing. "Look," one yelled, "he's humping the wall!"

Most of the kids in the pool were too young to be interested, but this group surrounded me and began to cheer me on.

"Do it again," one of them said.

"Yeah, show us how you hump the wall."

And all of them began to thrust their hips back and forth and make moaning sounds.

It felt weird and scary being surrounded

by all these older boys, and I looked around for someone to rescue me.

"You know what would make it feel even better?" one of the boys said, and before I knew what was happening, two of them were holding my arms while a third pulled off my bathing suit.

"Stop!" I screamed, kicking and writhing and contorting my six-year-old body in an effort to get free.

"Look at how tiny it is," one of the boys said. "I dare anyone to touch it."

And then a lifeguard was there, saying to leave the kid alone and giving me back my bathing suit and telling me to calm down and saying it was all just in fun. He took me out of the pool and gave me some candy, and when I had stopped crying, he told me to go back in the water and this time to make sure that I kept my bathing suit on. But the pool would never be the same. I spent the final few days of camp staring longingly at my spot on the wall and wondering whether I would ever find such happiness again.

Toward the end of the summer there was talk that the camp was facing a lawsuit, and

my parents started asking me a lot of
questions about our day-to-day activities.
I did not understand exactly what it was all
about, but I gathered it had something to do
with a popular activity the counselors had
invented for the younger campers called the
Coma Game.

Earlier in the summer, my counselor
explained to us what it meant to be in a
coma—no moving, no sound, basically being
dead. What we had to do was to imitate
someone in a coma, and the person who could
do the best imitation for the longest amount
of time would be the winner. Usually while
we played, our counselor would wander off
with the warning that he was watching us
from a secret hiding place. If he was in a
playful mood, he might come around and make
funny noises, and we would have to struggle
against laughter because people in comas
never laughed.

The problem came when Sammy Levy's
grandfather went into an actual coma.
Apparently Sammy had started making farting
noises when he visited his grandfather in
the hospital, and then asked his mother if

Grandpa could come with him to camp to show everybody how good he was at the Coma Game.

My parents seemed more amused than upset by the things I told them, and although they never sent me back to Camp Greenwood, the Coma Game became a staple in our household until I was old enough to realize how sick and twisted grown-ups really are.

NOVEMBER

When I get my first report card, there are no real surprises: Bs in history and Latin, B-minuses in science and math, a B-plus in American literature, and an A in Mr. Parke's writing seminar.

When my parents see my report card, they just shake their heads.

"I don't understand why someone as smart as you is getting Bs and B-minuses," my dad says.

I shrug. "Most of my classes are boring."

"Do you even care about getting into a good college?" my mom asks.

"I got an A in my writing class."

My mother gives me an exasperated look. "Good colleges expect you to be getting As in all your classes."

"Well maybe I won't go to a good college then," I say. "Maybe I'll just stay home and torture you instead."

"The hell you will." My father walks into the kitchen and pours himself a glass of scotch.

My mother frowns. "Are you drinking already? It's only five o'clock."

"Are you nagging already?" my father calls back. "It's only my first drink."

I walk to my room as they start their pre-dinner ritual.

My report card is not such a big deal. I mean I don't expect to get into an Ivy League school, and I know I'll get in somewhere. My parents are making me apply to a ridiculous number of colleges, twenty-three at last count, and I figure I have a realistic shot at about half of them.

They're crazy, my parents, and it's gotten worse with this whole college thing. We've been to visit almost every school in the Northeast, and my mom is constantly nagging me to start on my applications, which aren't due until the end of December.

I've actually finished a draft of an essay, though I'd never send it to a college admissions committee. Mr. Parke asked us to write something that would stand out from the thousands of essays the admissions people would be reading. He told us we were not allowed to write about any of our academic successes, describe any of our extracurricular accomplishments, discuss any of the people who have inspired us, or tell any stories about responsibility, independence, friendship, or discovering our true selves. So I wrote about my family.

I know that what I have written pushes boundaries and will make my parents hysterical if I show it to them. I know that my parents are already tense about my college prospects and that reading my essay will send them completely off their rockers. I know that the best course of action is to keep what I have written hidden in my folder until I turn it in to Mr. Parke tomorrow. But I just can't resist.

I stand in the doorway to the living room and watch my father trying to read the newspaper. He is pretending not to notice that my mother is very deliberately vacuuming the floor around his chair.

"I wrote a first draft of my college essay," I say.

My mother snaps off the vacuum and looks up. "Really? That's wonderful." She puts her hand on my father's shoulder. "Did you hear that, David?"

My father puts down the paper. "Atta boy."

"May I read it?" Mom asks.

I shrug. "It's still kind of rough."

"That's okay," Mom says. "Now we have plenty of time to work on it."

My parents are both ruthless when it comes to editing written work, which is why I stopped showing them my writing when I was in eighth grade.

"You promise to be nice?"

"No," my father says.

"David, stop that." My mother smiles at me. "Of course we'll be nice, sweetie."

I pretend to reread my essay. "I don't know," I say. "There's some stuff in here you might not like."

"It's a first draft," my mother says encouragingly. "It's not supposed to be perfect."

I hesitate a bit longer for dramatic effect, then, with a great show of reluctance, hand my paper to my mother, who grabs it and scurries off to her reading chair like a squirrel with a scrap of bread.

It takes a lot of self-restraint not to laugh as I watch my mother read, especially when she looks up at me with a horrified expression on her face.

"You can't write this," she says when she has finished.

I try to look insulted. "What do you mean?"

She thrusts the paper at my father. "Read this, David."

My father begins to read, smiles, then laughs out loud.

"It's not funny," my mother says angrily.

"It's hysterical," my father says.

"I didn't want to write an essay that would be like everyone else's," I say.

"Well, you certainly can't send this," my mother says.

"It's just a first draft."

My father looks up. "Oh, come on. You don't seriously think you can get away with this, do you?"

"You said it was hysterical."

"It is, but it's totally inappropriate."

"I don't think it's funny at all," my mother snaps.

"See, this is why I never show you any of my work," I say. "All you do is criticize."

My mom grabs the essay. "What do you expect when you write something like this?"

College Essay
First Draft

```
You think I've got it easy just
because I'm a white, upper-middle-class
Jew from New York? You think just
because I seem to have had every
advantage in life, I don't understand
true hardship? Let me assure you, I
know what it means to suffer. I know
what it means to feel pain.

    I still have vivid memories of the
time my father got my puppy drunk and
laughed when she threw up all over the
living room floor. Not to be outdone,
my mother later blackmailed me into
giving the dog away by moving out of
the house and refusing to return until
the dog was gone. My father forced me
to go to a baseball game, where I got
smashed in the face by a ball, and my
mother sent me off alone to visit my
mentally unstable grandmother, who had
```

already been hospitalized for mental illness seventeen times.

Do I sound like I'm complaining? Let me tell you about a typical dinner in my house. My father is drunk, of course, and my mother is venting her frustration in a passive-aggressive way that is making my father more and more irritated.

My mother is on a diet, so she has crackers and low-fat cottage cheese on her plate, but she keeps reaching over and taking bites of my father's food.

"Here," my father says, handing her his plate. "Just take it."

"Why are you so hostile?" my mother says. "I just wanted a bite."

"You've been picking at my plate since we sat down. All you ever do is pick, pick, pick."

"You have some real anger issues, don't you?"

My brother seems to be enjoying this little drama, but it is making me insane. "Enough already," I say. "Can we please eat dinner in peace for once?"

"There's no need to be scared, Shakespeare," my mother says. "A little conflict is healthy for a relationship. I wish you wouldn't suppress your feelings so much. Maybe therapy would—"

"I'm not going to therapy."

"It could really help you, Shakespeare."

"He needs a lot of help," my brother says. "You should see how antisocial he is at school."

"What the fuck's your problem?"

"You see?" my brother says. "Look how much pent-up anger he has."

He's right, you know. I do have a lot of pent-up anger. If I don't get out of my house soon, I'm likely to let all my grievances and resentments build up until they explode in some cataclysmic display of bloodshed and violence.

College is my only hope.

"Do you really feel this way?" my mother asks, this time with more concern than anger.

"It's a joke. It's supposed to be funny."

My mother seems deeply troubled, and I can't hold out any longer.

"I'm just messing with you. This isn't my real college essay. It's just an assignment for school."

"What?" My mother seems momentarily confused. "What kind of assignment? You turned this in?"

"You know," my father says, "I had totally forgotten about getting the dog drunk. That was pretty funny."

My mother gives me a stern look. "You can't joke about these things, Shakespeare. Kids are getting expelled for threatening violence."

"My teacher gave me an A," I lie. "He read it to the class."

"He read it to the class? David, did you hear that?" My mother is screaming now. "Oh my God, what are people going to think?"

"I kinda miss that dog," my father says.

My brother enters the room. "What's going on?" he asks. "Mom, what are you screaming about?"

"Nothing," my mother says, regaining her composure. "Go wash up for dinner."

We sit down to eat, and my mother asks my father to fix

her a stiff drink. I notice she makes a pointed effort not to touch the food on his plate during the meal.

The next day, Mr. Parke asks for volunteers to share their essays, and I raise my hand. Everyone applauds when I finish reading, and on the way out of class, Celeste asks me if I want to get together after school to give each other feedback on our memoirs.

"I think our strengths really complement each other," she says. "Your writing is just so . . . so . . . incendiary."

Incendiary? Any relation to Alejandero?

"We could work at my house," she says.

Hello. Now here is an interesting development. "That sounds good," I say.

She takes off her glasses, polishes them on her shirt, and puts them back on. "So I'll meet you at the lockers after school, okay?"

"Sounds good."

I spend the rest of the day vacillating between giddiness and extreme anxiety. By the time I meet Celeste, I feel ready to throw up.

"I have my mom's car," Celeste says as we walk outside. "My parents are away until tomorrow."

My stomach lurches, and I have to exert a tremendous amount of effort not to fart.

"How much of your memoir did you bring?" she asks.

"Just one chapter, the one about my dog. Everything else makes me look like a sexual deviant."

She laughs. "The dog your dad got drunk?"

"That's the one," I say.

It's a short drive, and soon we are sitting on the couch in Celeste's living room reading each other's memoirs.

"Your parents are hysterical," she says, flipping a page.

"Keep reading. It gets worse."

She looks up and smiles that disarming smile. "This reminds me of James Thurber. Have you read *My Life and Hard Times*?"

I shake my head. Who is this girl? She's like some kind of literary savant or something. I force myself to concentrate on the pages in front of me.

```
    The ambiguity of that night
imprinted a series of fragmented
images, which, when viewed through a
lens already distorted by time and
distance, leaves me hobbled in my
attempts to construct a truthful account
and to deconstruct my younger self.
```

"Who are you?" I mutter.

Celeste looks up, radiant. "That's it exactly," she gushes. She scoots closer to me so she can look at her paper. I feel her thigh press against mine. "Where are you?" she asks.

I put my finger on the word *ambiguity*.

She leans in closer, and I can feel her breath on my arm. "Is it clear what I'm trying to do?"

The words on the page blur together, and I have to remind myself to breathe. "I think so," I say. I don't look up. I don't move. And neither does she.

"What could I do to make it clearer?" she says at last.

Smaller words. Shorter sentences. Sit on my lap.

I turn my face and we begin to kiss.

Alejandero.

THE TIME MY MOTHER
USED EMOTIONAL BLACKMAIL
TO DEPRIVE ME OF
THE ONLY THING I EVER
REALLY WANTED

I had been begging for a dog for years, and finally, when I turned eleven, my parents relented.

The dog we picked out was brilliant. She was a newborn golden retriever, almost small enough to fit in the palms of my hands. She would slip and slide across the floor, urinate everywhere, and cry whenever she was left alone. I suggested we name her Killer.

"Here's the thing," my dad said. "Your mom and I never got the chance to name a girl, so we were thinking we would name the dog."

My mom nodded vigorously. "We've actually had a name in mind ever since Gandhi turned out to be a boy."

"No way. You're not giving this poor little puppy some freak name."

"You can't name her Killer," my mom said.

"She's my dog."

My dad pulled out his wallet. "How much will it cost to turn over the naming rights to us?"

"What? You're gonna pay me to let you name the dog?"

"How about twenty dollars? That seems fair."

"Are you serious?"

"Okay, we'll make it thirty."

"Thirty? You're gonna give me thirty dollars?"

"That's right."

I wondered if I could hold out for more, but decided not to press my luck. "Let me hear the name first," I said. "Then I'll decide."

My father hesitated and looked at my mother. She took a deep breath, then nodded.

"Onomatopoeia," my father said.

"Forget it. You're both insane."

My parents wore me down in the end by paying me the money and agreeing to move a

painting of a naked woman from the living
room into my bedroom.

The worst thing about owning a dog is
cleaning up her droppings. My parents had
insisted that if I wanted to keep
Onomatopoeia (whom I called Pee for short), I
had to take care of her. This meant feeding
her, walking her, and cleaning up after her.

"I don't want to see any dog shit in our
backyard," my dad said.

"And no letting her shit in the
neighbors' yards, either," my mom added.

I saw how other people cleaned up after
their dogs. They would take a paper or
plastic bag along, scoop up the droppings,
and carry their bag of feces to the nearest
garbage can. Clearly, this was out of the
question.

I approached Gandhi in his room that
night. "Mom told me to tell you that you
have to clean up after the dog from now on."

He did not even look up from the comic
book he was reading. "I'm not cleaning up
your dog's shit," he said.

I gritted my teeth. "All right, I'll pay
you."

He smiled, but still kept his eyes lowered. "How much?"

I hesitated. "A dollar a week."

He shook his head and laughed. "I'll do it for a dollar a turd."

"Are you crazy? That dog is a shitting machine."

Now he looked up for the first time. "Then make a counteroffer."

My brother had not yet turned ten, but already he was a cutthroat businessman who had amassed a small fortune through negotiations just like this one. His success hinged on his willingness to perform those tasks that others deemed too unpleasant to perform themselves. And there was absolutely nothing my brother would refuse, provided the price was right.

"Five dollars a week," I said.

My brother sighed. "Shakespeare, have you ever noticed that sometimes Pee's turds are a little bit wet and slimy?"

I felt my anger rising. "Fine, ten dollars, but I get to punch you every time I pay."

My brother pointed to a chart he had made

several months earlier after I had beaten him up and begged him not to tell our parents. "Three dollars per punch in the arm, ten dollars in the stomach, twenty dollars in the face."

I socked him as hard as I could in the arm and forked over thirteen dollars for the week.

Pee was my best friend, and with Gandhi responsible for cleaning up her shit, ours was a love with few complications. We played together, ate together, even slept together. One of my great pleasures was to climb into bed with wet feet and then lie back as Pee licked furiously at the water. I would squirm and giggle and let out an occasional shout.

"Stop molesting the dog," my father would call from the living room.

"It's called a foot massage!" I would shout back. "And the dog loves it."

One night my dad got drunk and spilled his beer. "C'mere, dog," he slurred.

Pee began to lick the floor. My dad stood propped against a wall and cheered her on.

"Jesus, Dad, she's just a puppy," I said.

Pee began to stagger around the house,

bumping into walls. Then she threw up on the living room floor.

"Clean up your dog's mess, Shakespeare," my dad said.

"You're the one who got her drunk."

"I'll do it," my brother said. "Five dollars."

There was nothing Pee wouldn't eat, but her absolute favorite food was my mother's brisket. She would sit motionless at my mother's feet as my mother cooked, staring up at her, and if my mother even glanced in her direction, she would begin to wag her tail furiously.

"No brisket," my mother would say. "Your dinner is in your bowl."

Pee's tail would thump and she would wriggle in excitement.

"Look," my mother would say, holding out her hands. "No brisket."

Pee would jump up and lick her empty hands.

"What do you want from me?" my mother would shout. "You're a dog! You're supposed to eat dog food!"

Pee would be in an absolute frenzy,

running around in circles and barking up at my mom.

"Oh, okay," my mom would say. "You can have brisket tonight, but this is the last time."

My mom was almost always the last one out of the house in the morning. When she would leave, Pee would press her face against the kitchen window so that if my mom turned around, even for an instant, she would see Pee staring at her.

Please don't leave me all alone, Pee's expression would say. Or at least that's how my mom interpreted it. And so my mom, racked with guilt, would abandon her plans and return inside.

"We have to give Onomatopoeia away," my mom announced at dinner one night.

I stopped eating mid-bite, a forkful of Mrs. Paul's fish sticks dangling in the air. "What? What are you talking about?"

"The Singletons have a huge farm and four dogs. Onomatopoeia will love it there."

"You've already talked to them? Dad, do you know about this?"

My father looked a little embarrassed.

"Your mother feels guilty leaving Onomatopoeia cooped up alone in the house all day. She's right, Shakespeare. Onomatopoeia will be happier with all that space to run around and all those dogs to play with."

"And you can visit her whenever you want," my mom added.

I shook my head vigorously. "No way. I've never asked for anything in my life except a dog. You can't just give her away."

"I can't go on feeling like a prisoner in my own house," my mom said.

"What do you go to therapy for?" I screamed.

"Maybe now isn't the best time to talk about this," my dad said.

Over the next few weeks, both my parents tried to broach the subject, but I was adamant. Pee was my dog, and I would not give her up.

In June, my mother went to Boston for the weekend to see friends. On Sunday night, she called and said she was going to stay a little longer. My father called me into his room.

"Your mother has decided not to come home until you agree to give Onomatopoeia to the Singletons."

"You're kidding, right?"

My father shook his head. "This is really a big deal to her, Shakespeare."

I guess I was too shocked to be very angry. Was my mother serious about not coming home? Had she been planning this all along or had she just decided to do it when she got to Boston? I had been to the Singletons' a few times. We had even brought Pee once, and she had galloped around the farm and played happily with the other dogs. Maybe it wouldn't be so terrible for her to live there. But there had to be something in it for me.

"What do you think?" my dad asked.

"I think Mom is crazy."

My father smiled. "Maybe, but the house feels kind of empty without her, don't you think?"

"I don't know," I said. "Let me think about it for a few days."

My father looked around and realized there was no alcohol in sight. "I like the dog, too," he said, "but a man gets lonely without his wife at night."

"Don't start that," I said. "That's playing dirty."

He smiled. "Your mother does this little thing—"

"AAAAH, I'M NOT LISTENING!" I screamed.

"Are we giving the dog away?" he asked.

"YOU'RE A HORRIBLE MAN!"

"Are we giving the dog away?"

"This is child abuse."

"Shakespeare, I'm about ten seconds away from telling you things that will haunt you for the rest of your life."

I've blocked what happened after that, but I remember that at some point my mother reappeared in the house, my dog vanished, and I had a second naked-woman picture hanging on my bedroom wall.

DECEMBER

So I'm currently working on the thirteenth draft of my real college essay. That's not an exaggeration. I told you my parents are crazy.

I'm also working on the twenty-sixth draft of a poem for Celeste. That is an exaggeration, but not by much. I'm crazy, too.

I never imagined going out with a girl would be so much trouble. Three weeks after our first kiss, I bring Celeste to the table where Neil, Katie, and I eat lunch every day. What a disaster! Celeste goes on and on, explaining the need for more diverse representation in the literary canon. Five minutes into it, I glance at Katie, who looks about ready to punch her in the face if she doesn't shut up.

Neil and Katie corner me later in the day by my locker.

"What's up with Celeste?" Neil asks. "Does she always talk like that?"

I shrug. "I guess. To be honest, half the time I have no idea what she's talking about."

"She better give unbelievable blow jobs for you to put up with that shit," Katie says.

"I wouldn't know," I say, feeling sheepish. "All we've done so far is kiss."

Katie stares at me in disbelief.

"We're just taking it slow," I say. I don't want to admit that every time I've tried to do more, Celeste has pulled away. I'm nervous that if I keep pushing, she'll dump me and file a restraining order.

"You've got to be the most pathetic person I know," Katie says.

"Whatever," Neil says. "At least you're getting something." He looks at Katie. "That's more than either of us can say."

Katie sneers. "You want to see what you're missing?" She takes Neil's head between her hands and kisses him long and hard on the mouth. Then she pushes him away.

"Wow," I say.

Neil is too stunned to move or speak.

"No big deal," she says, though her tone is softer and she seems to be trying to suppress a smile.

What I'm hoping is that if I write something for Celeste that she loves, she might be more open to my advances. So I started reading up on famous writers and jotting down funny observations about each one. Then I got bored and just started making things up. Twenty-six drafts later, here's what I have:

This poem, I do hope, is not an
    intrusion
I mean it to please, not disillusion.
I know of your deep love for
    literature
So forgive me for being a bit
    immature.

We can start way, way back with the
    epic bard Homer
Who wrote about Helen while nursing a
    boner.
And even though Homer was totally
    blind
He was blessed with something beyond a
    sharp mind.

Shakespeare (the first) while writing
    King Lear
Got totally hammered guzzling beer.
And in between poems, word has it that
    Keats
Liked to cavort betwixt oft-soiled
    sheets.

Milton himself was a mischievous louse
Whose favorite hobby was to egg
    Shakespeare's house.
And with whom did Milton engage in
    this fun?
Sometimes Ben Jonson, sometimes John
    Donne.

Dante's *Inferno* housed souls hot and
    sweaty,
But his own hell was worse after too
    much spaghetti.
Every great writer needs inspiration—
Dante's came from acute constipation.

Not many folks know that George
    Bernard Shaw
Could often be found wearing a bra.
And rumor has it that E. Allan Poe
Took a trip out to Walden to visit
    Thoreau.

Emerson looked on norms with defiance
While alone in his room he pursued
    self-reliance.
And many years later, there followed
    Ayn Rand

Who did more than write with that
    self-absorbed hand.

I don't know much philosophy, but I
    know that Descartes
Was renowned in his day for the way he
    could fart.
But even Descartes was not nearly as
    smelly
As that malodorous scoundrel Percy
    Bysshe Shelley.

I heard a recording of the brilliant
    James Joyce—
Did you know that the man had a real
    girly voice?
But Melville was manly, his neck was
    real thick,
He had hair on his back, and of course
    Moby-Dick.

In her great depression, Sylvia Plath
Neglected to take either shower or bath.
And while Spenser revised his great
    Faerie Queene

He failed to maintain good oral
    hygiene.

Dorothy Parker caused quite a stir
When her agent came over looking for
    her.
"Go away," she called out, "I'm
    fucking busy
And vice versa," she moaned in a
    delirious tizzy.

I thought I might take some time to
    peruse
A few books that were written by my
    fellow Jews.
I knew after reading *Portnoy's
    Complaint*,
Roth may be a Jew, but kosher he ain't.

And what about Isaac Bashevis Singer?
He didn't eat pork, but he sure was a
    swinger.
As a young man of twenty he shunned
    other Jews
And partied all night with his man
    Langston Hughes.

Winter nights in New Hampshire you
    could find Robert Frost
At the local saloon, where he liked to
    get sauced.
And in his spare time, old Joseph
    Heller
Liked making up jokes about Helen
    Keller.

Not many folks know that the great
    Norman Mailer
Grew up in Kentucky in the back of a
    trailer.
And while in Connecticut touring Mark
    Twain's,
I looked in his closet, saw handcuffs
    and chains.

I'm still trying to figure out how to end this thing. Maybe the reason it's so hard is that once I finish I know I will actually have to give it to Celeste, and I have no idea how she will react. Neil says if she doesn't like it, she's not worth dating in the first place. Katie says even if she does like it, she's not worth dating.

It's funny. The person I've been thinking who would really appreciate this poem is Charlotte White. We've become friend-lier over the past month, though with Charlotte it's hard to get too close. She comes to school late a lot, sometimes arriving during our morning math class, and always keeps herself at a bit of a distance from everything going on around her. Ms. Rigby has held her after class a few times, and she's seemed upset when she's come out, but when I've asked her about it, she's said it's nothing, just some work she owes.

One day I ask her to come sit with us at lunch. When I bring her to the table, Neil and Katie shoot me disbelieving looks and are uncharacteristically quiet throughout the meal. Charlotte does not seem to notice the stretches of silence, and she rarely speaks unless I address her point-blank. Several minutes before lunch ends, she excuses herself and slips out of the cafeteria.

"That girl freaks me out," Katie says.

"Why?" For some reason it feels important to me that Neil and Katie approve of her. "She's really nice," I say.

Katie shakes her head. "I don't know. She's better than your douche-bag girlfriend, but there's something off about her."

"How do you even know her?" Neil asks.

"She's in my math class, and we had English together last year."

"Does she have any friends?" Katie asks.

"I don't know," I say.

Katie picks up her tray and gives her leftovers to Neil. "Well, the next time you want to eat with her, do it somewhere else."

The next day on the way out of math class I ask Charlotte if she'll read something I've written.

"Sure," she says. "What is it?"

"I'll show you. Are you going to lunch?"

We walk to the cafeteria, get our gray hamburger patties, and find an empty table.

"Okay," I say, handing her the poem. "How would you react if someone gave you this? It's not finished, but you'll get the idea."

To my relief, she doesn't ask me who it's for or why I wrote it. She just accepts the paper and begins to read, and as she reads she begins to smile, and when she smiles I think to myself that she is actually rather attractive, not as obviously pretty as Celeste perhaps, but with a face that lights up unexpectedly and catches you by surprise.

"I'm shocked and offended," she says when she has finished, and we both laugh.

Then she says, "I think it's great."

I take the paper back. "Can I ask you something maybe a little bit personal?"

She takes on a guarded look.

"You don't have to answer," I say quickly. "I'm just wondering why you come late to school so much."

It takes a moment for her to relax, and even when she does, she still seems troubled. "I have to help out at home," she says at last, and even though I am consumed with curiosity, I know better than to press her.

* * *

Between thinking about Charlotte, playing boyfriend to Celeste, trying to finish my poem, arguing with my parents about college applications, and working on my memoir, I somehow manage to miss the moment when Neil and Katie move from being friends to being friends with benefits.

"Is something up with you and Katie?" I ask Neil as we walk out of school one day to catch the bus home.

Neil seems a bit uncomfortable. "What do you mean?"

"I don't know. You guys have just been acting a little weird lately."

Neil doesn't answer, and I feel a pit in my stomach.

"Tell me you're not sleeping with Katie."

"I'm not sleeping with Katie," Neil says quickly. His face is red.

"But you are doing other stuff." It's not so much a question as an accusation.

Neil does not say anything.

"You and Katie?" I am having trouble wrapping my mind around the concept.

"Well, you've been hanging out with Celeste so much."

"Not really. I have lunch with you guys almost every day."

Neil stops and faces me. "Are you angry?"

"No," I say angrily. "I just can't believe you've been doing it behind my back."

I don't know why this is all so upsetting to me. Am I

jealous? Why should I be when I have a girlfriend already? Am I worried about being the odd man out? Is it that I always imagined that if Katie ever went out with one of us it would be with me? Or is it just the shock of discovering that in the blink of an eye your whole sense of the universe can be turned upside down?

We get on the bus and take an empty seat near the back. "So how did all this happen?" I ask.

"You have to promise not to tell Katie I told you," Neil says. "She said if I tell anyone, she'll cut my balls off."

I promise, and Neil recounts how the day after that kiss in the cafeteria, they were hanging out at Katie's house, and Katie pulled out a bottle of vodka and they got drunk and then they just started kissing. "Since then, we've hooked up a few times, but Katie always wants to get drunk first."

When I get home, my brother and his girlfriend are in his bedroom with the door closed. I know they are in there, because I hear talking and giggling, and then Meredith's voice saying, "You first."

I hurry into my room, close the door, pull out the poem I have written for Celeste, read it over, and furiously compose a final verse:

```
These lines, I do hope, have been a
    diversion
And shown you more clearly my taste
    for perversion.
```

```
I wrote you this poem because I'm
    afraid
To come out and tell you I want to get
    laid.
```

I take a deep breath. I can't give her this. I cross it out, lie down on my bed, and close my eyes. I replay the experience of kissing Celeste for the first time. In my imagination, she takes my hand and leads me into her bedroom. We sit on her bed and kiss some more. I move my hand up her chest and she does not stop me. "Take off your pants," I whisper.

She looks at me and blushes. "You first."

I return to my poem and write a final verse.

```
Take pity, Celeste, on a struggling
    bard
My mind might be soft, but my pencil
    is hard.
My pen has been leaking all over my
    hand
Please be my paper; that would be
    grand.
```

On the day before Christmas vacation, Neil and Katie come to school hungover, Charlotte White does not come at all, and I come completely undone.

We are in Mr. Parke's class, and we have just submitted the next sections of our memoirs. Celeste has written about her political and ideological awakening, and I have written about getting caught in math class with a pornographic magazine.

"I wrote you something," I say at the end of class. I pull a folder from my book bag and hand her the poem.

I expect her to smile or to thank me or even to throw her arms around me and give me a kiss. Instead, she just stands motionless, not looking at the poem, but looking deeply troubled. "Shakespeare," she says at last, "we have to talk."

This does not bode well. It particularly does not bode well considering the final stanza of the poem I have just given her.

"This is really hard," she says.

Can we not do this in public, please?

"I really like you, Shakespeare."

No, you don't, or we wouldn't be having this conversation.

"I think we should just be friends."

Fine. Can I have my poem back?

"Are you okay?" she asks.

No. "I'm fine."

"We can still be friends, right?" she asks.

No. "Of course."

"I would still really love to read the poem."

"I don't think so," I say. I take the poem and walk out of the room.

I'm late to math, and the only open seat is in the front row.

Ms. Rigby gives me an annoyed look as I sit down. Normally, this would make me very uncomfortable. Today, I don't care. It is impossible to pay attention, and without realizing what I am doing I pull out the poem and begin to read it.

"What have you got there?" Ms. Rigby says, standing over my desk. "Give it to me."

My stomach lurches, and I feel history repeating itself. What is it about math class?

"I'll put it away," I say.

Ms. Rigby holds out her hand. "I said give it to me."

I do not have the stomach to get into a power struggle with a woman who has been intimidating her students for over twenty years. I hand her the paper. What the hell, I think. It's hard to imagine my day could get any worse.

She glances at it, then lays it on her desk and resumes teaching, her expression unchanged. After class, she tells me I am free to write whatever I want on my own time, but if I bring my smut into her room again she will contact my parents.

"That's all," she says when I do not leave right away.

"Can I have the poem back?" I ask.

She gives me a hard look. "I don't think so," she says, folding it up and putting it in her bag. "Have a nice vacation."

THE TIME I GOT CAUGHT WITH A PORNOGRAPHIC MAGAZINE IN MATH CLASS

I have never really understood the social dynamics of the classroom, but it seems to operate along the same lines as a dog run. You have all the regular dogs who come to the dog run each day, and then, every once in a while, a new dog arrives on the scene. When this happens, all the regular dogs stop whatever they're doing and rush to sniff the new dog's butt.

So it was when Will Baker arrived on the first day of seventh grade. He was one of those small-limbed, sandy-haired, freckle-faced boys, who looks just innocent enough to make you nervous. All through the day, groups of girls would surround him with a million questions, then hurry off, giggling and whispering.

I didn't actually hear what the girls were asking, but I felt pretty sure that they were trying to determine his answers to such thought-provoking questions as whether he had a girlfriend, whether he wanted a girlfriend, and who in the class he thought was cute. It was more than a little disconcerting, then, when Lisa Kravitz and Stacey McCaber turned around and stared at me, then rushed away, giggling like a pair of demented hyenas.

Will shrugged his shoulders, as if he didn't have any idea what the girls were carrying on about, but I could barely concentrate for the rest of the day.

I caught up with him after school and introduced myself.

"That's your real name?" he asked in disbelief.

"My parents are crazy," I said.

He nodded. "That's cool."

"What were those girls giggling about in class?" I was most interested in finding out about Lisa Kravitz, a childhood friend I was secretly in love with.

He shrugged. Then, in a conspiratorial whisper: "Hey, you want to see something?"

"What?"

He unzipped his book bag and pulled out a magazine.

My eyes popped as I looked at the cover. "Jesus, where did you get that?"

He stuffed it back in his bag. "I got a lot of them."

I looked around and lowered my voice. "Let me see that again."

Will smiled. "You want it? I'll sell it to you."

"How much?"

He looked me up and down. "I'll give you a good deal. Ten dollars."

"Ten dollars? That's too much."

"You don't want it? Fine with me."

All night I thought about that picture on the cover of the magazine. Even though I had paintings of naked women in my room, they were nothing like what Will had shown me. It occurred to me that if I bought the magazine, my parents would probably find it, and I would have to escape to a cave in

Tibet to live out my days in utter
humiliation. It's not that I would get in
trouble. My parents didn't really believe in
punishment. No, what would happen would be
far worse: They would want to talk about it.

"Where did you get this magazine?" they
would ask. "Do you enjoy looking at these
pictures? It's normal, you know, for boys
your age to think about these things. Do you
have any questions you want to ask us?"

I bought the magazine the next day.

It turned out that Will had lots of
magazines, and he soon established a
profitable little business.

We quickly became friends out of mutual
need. I needed someone who raised my cool
quotient and improved my chances of
impressing Lisa, and he needed someone who
would follow him around like a lost puppy
and do whatever he said.

"Where do you get all these?" I once
asked him.

"Steal 'em," he said.

"What? How? Where?"

"Stores, magazine stands. It's no big
deal."

"Oh my God, I'm friends with a criminal."

He gave me a dirty look. "You better not say anything."

My voice took on an increased sense of urgency. "Aren't you afraid of getting caught? They put kids in jail these days."

"Chill out. I'm not gonna get caught."

I realized that if Will ever got caught while I was with him, I would probably be named as an accomplice. Everyone in town would read about it in the paper, and for the rest of my life, wherever I moved I would have to register with the police as a convicted sex offender.

Meanwhile, I had plenty of other things to worry about, first and foremost making sure no one discovered the magazine I had bought. I had agonized for days over the best place to hide it. The problem was that no matter where I put it, I was able to come up with a perfectly plausible scenario in which someone would find it. I had stuck it between the box spring and the mattress of my bed the first night, but then I thought, What if my brother and his friends start jumping up and down on all the beds in the house and mine collapses? Then they try to put it back together, and . . . hello, what's this? So I buried the magazine in my closet, then hid it behind a picture, then put it inside an old notebook on my shelf. But no matter where I put it I knew deep down that the only sensible course of action was to get rid of it as soon as possible.

Of course, this was totally out of the question. The women in the magazine had become more familiar to me than my own family. There was Marina, who had short blond hair and enjoyed going to the movies and riding motorcycles. Then there was Angela, who liked to travel and go skinny-dipping in the ocean. Will had offered to sell me other magazines at a discount because we were friends, but I felt a fierce loyalty to the women I had come to know. Didn't Patricia, on page eighty-seven, say that loyalty was one of the qualities she most looked for in a man?

One woman who could legitimately compete for my affections was Ms. Mitchell, who looked more like an Amazon warrior than a seventh-grade math teacher. She was young and tall and blond and strong and, miracle of miracles, not yet married. But more than anything, what made her so incredibly desirable was the fact that she liked me. I knew this because she always smiled at me and asked me to solve the hardest problems on the board, and because sometimes she would put her hand on my shoulder while she was walking around the room.

I had always been a good math student without really trying, but with Ms. Mitchell I applied myself as I never had before. In class I would find myself staring at her in rapt attention and wondering how it was that I never before had seen the beauty of a mathematical equation.

It was inconceivable, then, that I would jeopardize my relationship with Ms. Mitchell by bringing my pornographic magazine to her class, and not just bringing it in, but actually taking it out while she was teaching. Unfortunately, sometimes things happen in life that are simply beyond your control.

The night before the fateful incident, my mother announced that she had hired a cleaning service to come in the next day. The house was a mess, she said, and it needed professional attention. I couldn't risk having the cleaners find my magazine, so I stuffed it in my book bag to bring to school. Then Will pulled me aside at school and said there was a rumor that the principal was going to inspect the lockers.

"I have my magazine. Where am I supposed to put it?" I whispered.

"Just keep it in your book bag. I've got, like, ten in mine."

Every time I had to open my bag to take something out or put something away, there was the magazine staring me in the face. By the time I got to math class, I was a nervous wreck. In math the desks were pushed together for cooperative learning, and when I opened my bag to get my book, Rocco Mackey somehow saw inside.

"Dude, is that a porno?" he whispered. Rocco Mackey was repeating seventh grade and had the IQ of a doorknob.

"Shhh. We're in class."

"Let me see it."

I had to do something fast, or Rocco might begin to salivate. "Just be quiet. I'll show you after school."

He nodded. "Where?"

I tried to ignore him, but he tugged on my shirt.

"Outside the school, now shut up."

Ms. Mitchell looked ravishing that day, but I was such a basket case all I could do was pray for the end of class to come quickly. We were supposed to be working with our partners on a set of problems, which usually meant me doing them, Rocco drawing obscene pictures in his notebook, and then Rocco copying what I had written.

"Dude, she's not looking," Rocco whispered. "Let me see the magazine."

"Not now, we're supposed to be working." I could feel the sweat pooling under my armpits.

Ms. Mitchell moved around the room. "Do I have a volunteer to put number one on the board?" She looked at me expectantly, and I felt myself blush.

"How about it, Shakespeare?"

Normally, I would have been delighted to do anything Ms. Mitchell asked of me, but I was terrified of leaving my bag unguarded for even a second.

"I don't think I got that one right," I muttered.

She looked at my paper. "That's right," she said. "Go ahead and put it up. Who wants to put up number two?"

I gave Rocco my most threatening look, walked to the front of the room, copied the problem as quickly as possible, and hurried back to my seat. My book bag was unzipped, and the magazine was gone.

I looked over at Rocco. He was slouched in his chair, staring at his lap with his eyes popped out and his tongue making circles around his lips, looking for all the world like a starving boy with a big juicy steak in front of him.

There was no question that something disastrous was going to happen. Any moment now, Ms. Mitchell would turn away from the board, see Rocco drooling on himself, and discover the magazine. It occurred to me that if I got expelled from school, at least

I wouldn't have to do the science project that was due next week.

"Give it back," I whispered through gritted teeth.

"Shhh, don't draw attention to me."

In desperation, I grabbed for the magazine, Rocco grabbed my wrist, both our hands banged into the desk, and everyone in the class turned to stare at us.

Ms. Mitchell was there in two Amazonian strides. "Give me the magazine," she said. When she saw what it was, she blushed deeply and seemed at a total loss for what to do.

"It's not mine," Rocco said. "You can ask him."

Ms. Mitchell looked ready to explode. "Both of you need to come with me to the principal's office right now!" She turned to the class. "Start on your homework. And if I hear a sound from this room, you'll all have detention tomorrow."

We didn't get expelled. The principal listened to Ms. Mitchell, then asked us a bunch of questions, then gave us a long lecture, then called our parents to come pick us up. I told the principal exactly what had happened, the only lie being that I had found the magazine on the way to school that day.

We waited outside the office for our parents to show up, and Rocco started to cry. "I'm so dead," he said. "My dad said if he caught me reading pornos again, he'd send me to military school."

My father arrived first, and he looked more concerned than angry. He spoke to the principal for a few minutes, then told me we were going home.

"Are you okay?" he asked after we were in the car.

"I guess so."

"That must have been really embarrassing in class."

"I'm never setting foot in that school again."

My father laughed. "Your principal showed me the magazine. I can see why math must seem pretty boring in comparison."

I didn't really want to talk about porno magazines with my father, because anything he said was bound to be disturbing.

"You know, I used to read magazines like

that," he said. "But then I met your mother and she—"

"Okay, Dad, I don't need to hear that. Does Mom know what happened?"

"Your principal called her first, then Mom called me and told me I had to go to school because she was too embarrassed."

My mother is one of those people who lives and dies by what people might think. It wouldn't have been a big deal to her to find out that I was reading pornographic magazines, as long as nobody else knew. For her, the great tragedy was that I had been caught, and now people she knew would talk about what had happened.

"Why couldn't you just look at your magazine inside the house?" she asked over and over at dinner that night.

"I can't believe you never showed it to me," my brother said.

Will called me later that night to find out what had happened. "You didn't tell anyone where you got the magazine, did you?"

I assured him I had not.

"Thanks," he said. "I'll give you another one for free tomorrow."

"No thanks," I said. "I'm trying to convince my parents to transfer me to another school."

My parents made me go back to school the next day. Word had gotten around about what had happened, and for one day I actually experienced what it was like to be popular. I gave Ms. Mitchell an apology note at the beginning of math class, and she told me that writing the note was a very mature thing to do and that she was glad to have me back.

On my way out of school, I saw Will Baker and Lisa Kravitz kissing in the stairwell.

JANUARY

Here's a little multiple-choice quiz.

Why did Celeste break up with me?
a) She was more comfortable with our
   just being friends.
b) She was never really interested in
   me and only needed a little
   diversion to get her mind off
   Jordan Miller.
c) Jordan Miller came home from
   college for Christmas vacation, and
   she went rushing back to him.
d) She is manipulative and selfish,
   with no qualms about trampling on a
   poor boy's heart.
e) All of the above, especially d.

What happens is I go to the movies with Neil over vacation and there they are, at the concession stand, buying buttered popcorn. They are holding hands, and Celeste is looking radiant. When she sees me, she whispers something to Jordan, and he looks at me and nods.

Celeste leaves Jordan in line and walks over.

"Hi," she says.

"Hey." I really do not want to talk to her.

"How are you?"

I shrug. "I'm okay."

She looks around. "Are you here alone?"

"Neil's in the bathroom."

We stand there in silence. Can't she sense that this is an uncomfortable situation, or is she just too caught up in her newfound happiness to recognize the misery she has caused me?

"I feel like vacation started, and we never really had proper closure," she says.

I look toward the bathroom. Where the hell is Neil? Why does he always have to take a crap before every movie? "It's okay," I say. "It wasn't meant to be."

Jordan calls out to Celeste, and I use the moment to say good-bye and slip off into the theater. Neil and I have come to see *Bloody Battle II,* and I am more than ready for some graphic violence and gratuitous bloodshed.

I spend most of vacation finishing up college applications, working on my memoir, stressing out about the poem Ms. Rigby has confiscated, seething with resentment, and feeling sorry for myself. On New Year's Eve, I get drunk with Neil and

Katie, make a clumsy pass at her, vomit, and end up passing out on the bathroom floor. Three days later, school resumes.

I sit as far away from Celeste as I can the first day back. I want her to feel guilty. I want her to feel rejected. I want to win the memoir award and I want her to lose. I want her to realize what she has given up. I want her to beg me for another chance and I want to tell her she had her chance and blew it. She catches my eye during class and smiles. I smile back.

Mr. Parke returns our writing. He writes on my paper that the humor is wonderful, but I am using it as a defense mechanism to avoid confronting myself in a more substantive and honest way. He says I need to spend time reflecting on who I am and why I always cast myself as the victim in my life's story. He sounds a lot like my mother. She's been pushing me for years to see a therapist.

My mother is a great believer in therapy. She is also a vegetarian, a practitioner of yoga, and an aspiring Buddhist. Since therapy has performed such wonders for her—or so she claims—she is convinced that it could also perform wonders for me.

"It could change your life," she is always saying.

"Maybe it could," I say. "We'll never know."

"Why are you so resistant?"

And my standard reply: "I don't know. I bet a therapist could help me figure that out."

The truth is I know exactly why I'm resistant. I don't want

a therapist to tell me things about myself I don't want to hear, and I don't want to admit that I have problems I can't deal with myself. It would be one thing if I could just go in and complain about my life, but having to confront and take responsibility for my shortcomings and insecurities is something I have no interest in.

Charlotte has been in and out since we came back to school. She always looks tired, and she is always working during lunch, probably trying to make up all the assignments she's missed.

"Is everything okay?" I ask her about a week after we've returned. It is the end of the day, and she is slumped against her locker with her head resting on the door.

She quickly stands. "I'm just tired."

What is she hiding? I wonder. Why does she keep herself so closed off? I ask her how her memoir is coming.

"Slowly." She looks at the floor and pushes her hair out of her face. "It's opening up a lot of things that are hard to write about."

"I know what you mean," I say. "My life's been one disaster after another."

She gives me a sad smile.

"Do you want to get together sometime and give each other feedback on our memoirs?" I ask.

This seems to catch her off guard, and she takes a moment

to answer. "I don't know. Maybe when we know each other a little better."

The crowd by the lockers is thinning out. I spy Lisa Kravitz making her rounds, exchanging greetings and good-byes with everybody, and when she sees me she flashes a wonderful smile and waves. "Hey, Shakespeare," she says, walking over.

I say hi, and Charlotte smiles.

"I'm Lisa," she says, extending her hand. "We haven't met, but I've seen you around. Charlotte, right?"

Charlotte nods, surprised.

"Lisa knows everybody," I say.

"It's nice to meet you," Charlotte says, turning to her locker to finish packing her book bag.

"How are you?" Lisa asks me.

"I'm okay."

A group of her friends walks past and calls out to her. "Let's talk soon," she says, squeezing my arm and bounding off to catch up with them. I turn back to Charlotte, who has finished packing her bag.

"I'll see you," she says. "I need to get home."

I realize I have never seen Charlotte outside of school, and I ask her where she lives.

She hesitates. "We kind of move around a lot."

What does that mean? I wait for her to say more, but she just turns and walks off down the hall.

The second quarter is ending next week. The night before my history final I come down with a big cold, sleep miserably, and wake up feeling like someone has opened a fire hydrant inside my nose. My parents don't believe in staying home from school for anything less than the plague, so I pop a couple of Sudafed and set off for what I am sure will be a wretched day.

I'm one of those people who, instead of blowing my snot into a tissue, sucks it back up into my nostrils. It works really well except when I suck too hard and feel the snot shoot all the way back into my throat, and then I have to run to a sink or toilet to spit it out.

"Don't suck it back in," my parents are always scolding me. "You have to blow it out."

My father is a tremendous nose-blower. He always carries a handkerchief in his pocket, and several times a day he pulls it out and unleashes a mighty roar. Then he uses the handkerchief to dab at any stray snot or pick at any loose boogers, before putting the whole gloppy mess back in his pocket.

"Why don't you carry a handkerchief in your pocket?" my father asks.

"You have a box of tissues in your bedroom," my mother says. "What do you think they're for?"

I know perfectly well what they're for, but I'm certainly not going to discuss that with my mother.

"You sound like a snorting pig," my brother says.

It is true that I occasionally get dirty looks from people when I snort too loudly, but it has become second nature and most of the time I don't even realize I am doing it.

We have history first period, and Mr. Mullen hands out blue books for us to write our answers in. His tests always consist of a single essay question that requires us to take a position on some big topic and back up our ideas with specific historical detail.

His primary interests are weapons, wars, and military strategy. He always tells us that his greatest disappointment in life is that a heart condition kept him out of the army when he was younger, and he often likes to conduct simulated battles in the classroom to demonstrate his military genius.

I lift the test paper to read so I won't have to lean over and give my snot the added advantage of gravity in trying to escape. The test question is predictable:

What was the biggest military mistake made by each side during the Civil War? Be sure to include the names of specific people, locations, regiment numbers, and weapons in your response. (Note: I am not interested in hearing your opinions about the causes or consequences of the war.)

The moment I start to write I feel the snot begin to drip and I give a violent snort, hoping to beat back the charge before it can really get going. There is definite strategy involved here. The trick is to snort at times when I won't call undue attention to myself: when somebody coughs, for example, or when somebody moves his or her chair. What I don't count on is such a persistent line of attack, and before I realize what I am doing I am working overtime to keep the enemy forces at bay.

I guess it must be frustrating trying to concentrate on an important test and having to listen to someone snorting up snot every few seconds. Still, I am completely blindsided by Paige Blanchard's strike from all the way across the classroom.

"Would you just blow your nose!" she screeches. "That's so unbelievably annoying."

Everybody in the class looks up, a few people laugh, and somebody says, "Thank you, Paige."

Mr. Mullen seems amused by the whole scene. "Go get some tissues, Shakespeare," he says.

I can feel the eyes on me as I hurry from the room, trying desperately to make it out before any snot leaks down my face.

Safe in a bathroom stall, I wipe my nose with toilet paper and feel the full weight of my humiliation come crashing down. Not only is Paige Blanchard one of the most desirable girls in the school, she is also best friends with Jody Simons, the top girl on my fantasy list. Once Jody hears about this, any tiny possibility that she might be interested in me will be irrevocably destroyed.

I can't stay in the stall forever, but the thought of going back to class is almost more than I can bear. In the first place, everybody will look up when I come back in the room. Then there is the problem of what to do about my nonstop runny nose. I have barely started my essay, and there are now only thirty minutes left in the period. I stuff as much toilet paper as I can in my pocket, take a gigantic snort, and hurry back to class.

Once at my desk, I devise a system that I think will keep my snot at bay. What I do is put my non-writing arm across my desk and slouch so my nose and mouth are pressed against the sleeve of my shirt. In this position, my eyes are right up close to my test paper, my writing hand is free, and I have formed a barrier against the onslaught of snot cascading from my nose. It is a bit difficult to breathe, no question about that, and I am aware that snot is pooling up against my sleeve, but I manage to make it through the rest of the period without causing any more of a racket.

"Time's up," Mr. Mullen says. "Turn in your tests on your way out."

There is a lot of commotion as students push away from their desks, gather their things, and begin to move around the room. I lift my face gingerly from my arm and realize that my sleeve is drenched with snot, and my whole lower face feels sticky and wet. Most appalling is that as I raise my face, I trail a string of snot that stretches up with me from my sleeve, so I have to bury my face quickly again in my shirt before anyone notices.

I grab the wad of toilet paper in my pocket and try to raise my face and wipe it simultaneously. The snot is mounting a final, vicious attack, coming at me from all sides and overwhelming my defenses. The situation is desperate. I have to beat a hasty retreat to the bathroom or all will be lost. The key is not to make eye contact with anybody, to keep my head down, to drop my test book on Mr. Mullen's desk with one hand, to cover my mouth and my nose with the other, and to make a beeline for the bathroom.

All this I accomplish, though I can only imagine how pathetic and ridiculous I look to the groups of students crowding the hallway. What's even worse is that Mr. Parke's class begins in three minutes.

I stand in the bathroom stall for the second time in the past hour. My nose is running, and I feel awful. Why the hell did I come to school today? I want to be home in bed. I want to get as far away from what just happened as possible. There's certainly no way I can sit through another class.

I make my way to the office, call my mother, and get permission to sign out. It is thirteen degrees outside, even colder with the wind. As I push away from the school building, I see someone who looks like Charlotte coming toward me, walking slowly up the street with her head down.

"You're late," I say as she reaches me.

She looks up, startled. Her eyes are wet, but I can't tell if this is from the wind or if she has been crying.

"Are you okay?" I ask.

She wipes her eyes and nods. "Where are you going?" she asks.

"Home. I signed out because I'm sick."

She looks up at the school building, and I can tell she doesn't want to go any farther. It seems like it has been a great effort for her just to make it here. Should I invite her back to my house? If only I didn't feel so sick.

"I should go," she says, but she doesn't move.

It's freezing, and my nose is starting to run. I give a violent snort and rub my nose with my hand. I feel bad walking away, but I can't endure a repeat of this morning's performance.

"I'll see you," I say. I hurry toward the bus stop without turning around, wondering the whole way if Charlotte is watching me.

I get home and take my temperature: 101.5. My mother comes home later and finds me in bed. She makes me soup, but I have no appetite. My brother says I probably have mono. He actually seems concerned. Then the phone rings and he goes off to talk to his girlfriend. I feel nauseated.

It ends up being a mild case of the flu. I am out of school for two more days and go through three boxes of tissues, which I use to wipe up various bodily fluids. Neil comes by to see how I am, to compare bowel movements, and to complain about Katie, who he says is an alcoholic. I tell him about my history-class fiasco and ask him how I am supposed to show my face in school again.

"Relax," he says. "I'm sure you're the only one still thinking about it."

"I bet Paige told Jody."

"You're so paranoid."

I wipe my nose. "What do you expect?"

"Trust me," he says. "Paige Blanchard has better things to do than sit around talking to her friends about your runny nose."

This might be true, but I have no doubt that something bad will come of all this. If there's one thing my experiences have taught me, it's always to expect the worst.

I tread warily into history my first day back and try to make myself invisible. I am convinced that everybody is thinking about what happened three days earlier. Every glance in my direction feels like a bullet, every cough or sneeze like a live grenade. At the end of class, I pack my books quickly and try to escape before the rush, but Paige Blanchard cuts me off.

"How are you feeling?" she asks.

My face burns. "I'm okay," I mutter without looking at her. Why is she doing this to me? She's never spoken to me before.

"I'm sorry about the other day," she says. "It was just so hard to concentrate."

Please, stop talking about it. "It's okay."

I push on and out of the classroom before any more damage can be done. Obviously, the incident has not been forgotten. People have been talking about it, the story has been told and retold, my social status has been downgraded from sad to seriously pathetic, and I am now destined to spend the remainder of my high school career avoiding Paige Blanchard.

I walk into Mr. Parke's class. The next chapters of our memoirs are due, and Mr. Parke asks if anybody would like to share what they have written. There is no way I am going to share. I have written about being hit in the face by a baseball at a Yankees–Red Sox game, but the story also includes details of my rampant paranoia, my harrowing experience in a public urinal, my arousal at witnessing a drunken catfight, and—irony of all ironies—my goddamn leaky nose.

"No volunteers?" Mr. Parke says.

I look up and see Rocco Mackey staring at me and smiling. This does not bode well.

THE TIME I GOT HIT IN THE FACE BY A BASEBALL AT A YANKEES-RED SOX GAME

A few weeks before my fourteenth birthday, my father announced that he had bought tickets to a Yankees-Red Sox game. I didn't want to go, because I was convinced I would get hit in the face by a ball. My father told me I was being ridiculous, that the odds of a ball even coming near me were a thousand to one, and that if, by some slim chance, a ball did come in my direction, I should stick up my glove and try to catch it.

"Do you have any idea how fast those balls come at you?" I asked.

"Shakespeare, millions of people go to baseball games every year. Do you really think they would all go if it was dangerous?"

"Millions of people fly on airplanes, too," I said.

"Airplanes are one of the safest ways to travel."

"Come on, Dad, don't tell me you actually believe that propaganda."

My father picked up his newspaper, a signal that he didn't have the energy to argue with me at the moment.

I ignored the signal. "Millions of people own guns, millions of people smoke cigarettes, millions of people swim in the ocean and risk getting eaten by sharks."

He didn't look up, so I walked into the kitchen and started to bother my mother.

The reason we were going to the baseball game in the first place was because my father was determined to do all those father-son activities his father had never done with him. It didn't matter that I didn't want to go. What mattered was that my father had had a lousy childhood, and he was not going to make the same mistakes that his parents had made.

The contempt my parents had for their parents was basically what shaped their philosophy of child rearing. It was simple. They made decisions by doing the opposite of what their parents had done. Their parents had given them common names, David and Sarah, so they gave us the most unusual names they could come up with. Their parents had made lots of rules, so they were raising us with as few rules as possible. Their parents had never taken them to baseball games, so they would take us to baseball games whether we liked it or not.

Actually, my mother decided that my father could take us to the baseball game on his own. Not only did she have no interest in baseball, but she also happened to be terrified of cars, especially cars driven by my father. When she absolutely had to be in the car, she would sit in the backseat with her eyes squeezed shut and a miserable look on her face. If we were going on a long trip, she would wedge herself onto the floor in the back and put her head on the seat, covered by a blanket.

It was a miracle that we made it to the stadium alive. My father is one of those men who thinks he's a much better driver than he actually is. In fact, I would have to say that my father is probably one of the ten worst drivers I know. At least it was early enough in the day that I knew he was sober.

Neither my brother nor I wanted to sit in the front, so we flipped a coin, and I ended up in the death seat.

We had barely left our house when a car honked at us. My father had switched lanes without looking in his rearview mirror, one of many habits that made me wonder why the state had not yet revoked his license.

"It helps if you look first," my brother said.

My father turned quickly around. "I don't need any backseat driving."

"Will you watch the road?" I screamed.

My dad began to fiddle with the radio. What went through my head was that if we died, at least I wouldn't get hit in the face by a ball at the baseball game.

"Do the air bags work?" I asked.

My father ignored me.

We hit traffic as we approached Yankee Stadium, and my dad kept lurching into different lanes that he thought were moving faster, and then lurching back when he realized he should have stayed where he was in the first place. It was hard to believe that so many people could be going to one baseball game, and I felt a twinge of hope that maybe the game would be almost over by the time we got there. I said a silent prayer, then grabbed the seat as my dad lurched into the next lane and cursed under his breath as it came to a complete stop.

I don't know if it was all the traffic or the fact that my father hadn't had any alcohol yet that day, but he was a jangle of nerves by the time we got to the stadium.

"Stick close," he said. "I don't want anyone getting lost in the crowd."

My dad had a habit of losing me. It stretched all the way back to when I was four and he lost me in a cemetery while he was jogging and I was riding my Big Wheel. Then there had been the incident at the amusement park when I was eight and the hiking trip when I was ten. I wondered whether I should start a list of all the grievances I had against my parents; there was certainly a large possibility that this day would come to figure prominently in my litany of complaints against my dad.

Our seats were in the bleachers, which, my father said, was where the real fans sat. As far as I could tell, these were the cheapest seats in the stadium, and I quickly realized that the people who chose to sit in the bleachers were the people who needed to save as much money as possible for beer.

The game had barely begun, and most of the people around us were clearly drunk. A player for the Red Sox was at bat, and the guys behind us, who were shirtless and had painted their chests to spell out YANKEES, started an obscene chant. I wondered what my father was thinking, but he was completely preoccupied with trying to get the beer vendor to notice him.

"Isn't this great?" he said once he had paid eight dollars for a plastic cup of Budweiser. "You guys want some hot dogs?"

"I'll take a wiener," my brother said, and he started to giggle like an idiot.

"You suck, Red Sox," the guys behind us

started to yell, and everybody around us took up the chant. "You suck, Red Sox. You suck, Red Sox."

I put my fingers in my ears, but my father quickly knocked them out. "These guys will kill you if you don't join in."

So now, in addition to worrying about getting hit by a baseball, I needed to act like a Neanderthal or risk getting torn apart. On the bright side, if I got killed at the baseball game, at least I wouldn't have to drive home with my father. I looked over at him and saw he was now licking the inside rim of his empty beer cup.

The game was moving along at a snail's pace, and I had to go to the bathroom. I had mixed feelings about this. If I went to the bathroom I would be safe from any baseballs flying in my direction. On the other hand, I was likely to get lost if I went off by myself. I decided to wait until my father needed to go, which, at the rate he was drinking, wouldn't be long.

"Who needs to take a leak?" my father asked about thirty seconds later.

I've never liked public restrooms, but

this one had to be the worst I'd ever seen. The smells of beer and urine assaulted me as I walked in, beer cups and toilet paper were strewn across the floor, and there was a mass of drunk people standing in line waiting to use the urinals. I considered waiting for a stall so I could have some privacy, but I couldn't risk what might be floating in the toilets.

My turn came, and I stepped up to the plate. The man to my left was making little moaning noises and the man to my right was leaning forward with one hand against the wall to keep himself upright. I pushed myself as close to the urinal as possible and concentrated, but nothing would come. This always happened to me when I had to urinate in public. I tried to block out all the distractions around me, and finally I felt the beginnings of a trickle. The man on my left finished, and my father took his place.

Now, if there's one thing that I don't need to see, it's my father's penis. He might have considered this a wonderful father-son bonding moment, but I was mortified, especially when I saw that he was trying to sneak a peek at my little friend. I angled my body to block his view, finished as quickly as I could, and stepped away. A few drops of urine dribbled down my leg. Somebody—probably my father—farted loudly.

It was the bottom of the ninth inning and the Red Sox were winning by one run. I was less concerned with the score than with the fact that so far no balls had been hit into the bleachers. By the law of averages, I was now sitting in one of the most dangerous parts of the stadium.

The first batter for the Yankees stepped up to the plate.

On the huge screen broadcasting the game, the picture jumped from the batter to a bunch of hysterical, chest-painted fans holding up a sheet with a bull's-eye painted on it.

"Oh crap," I said, swinging around and spilling Coke all over myself.

"Hey, we're on TV!" my brother screamed.

Everybody around me was waving like crazy for the camera. They were jumping up and making faces and pointing at the screen, and since most of them were totally drunk, they were knocking into each other and creating a scene of total chaos. The camera had already jumped back to the batter, but the commotion in our section was just beginning. One large drunk man accidentally knocked into the drunk girlfriend of another large drunk man, and she began to curse him out at the top of her lungs. Then the drunk girlfriend of the first drunk man stepped forward and began to shout curses back, and all the other large drunk men in the section began to whoop and cheer and scream.

"Catfight!" someone yelled, and the chant was taken up, broken only by a few screams of "Take it off!"

I had never seen women fight before, and I found the spectacle oddly exhilarating. Without realizing it, I had taken up the chant with the crowd and was standing on my seat to get a better view of the action. Policemen were rushing up the aisle, but it was taking them a long time to get through the mass of large drunk men who had formed a ring around the female combatants.

Nobody around me was watching the game,

so nobody saw the pitcher rear back and
throw, the batter step forward and swing,
and the ball jump off the bat and hurtle
through the air. When the crowd roared, we
turned to find the outfielders running back.
The people around me began to scream and
make lunging movements. The ball glanced off
somebody's glove, ricocheted into my face,
and fell to the ground. My brother pounced,
and suddenly there we were on the big
screen, my brother holding the ball
triumphantly, and me, next to him, with a
dazed look on my face and blood dripping
from my nose.

The game ended up going to extra innings
before the Yankees finally won. Everybody
said it was one of the best games of the
season, and they kept showing highlights on
all the sports shows. We weren't there when
the game ended, though. My nose was spurting
so much blood that my father rushed me to
the stadium's medical station, where they
patched me up. My father made some dumb
jokes to try to get me to laugh, and my
brother even offered me the baseball. The
thing is, I wasn't really that upset. I had

been so sure a baseball would hit me and
that when I got hit I would lose sight in
one eye or break a bone in my cheek that I
felt lucky to be escaping with just a bloody
nose.

My mother, who had watched the whole game
on television hoping to catch a glimpse of
us, was beside herself by the time we got
home. I let her make a fuss over me for a
while and cook my favorite meal, lasagna. At
dinner that night, she sprung the good news.
My mentally unstable grandmother had sent me
a plane ticket to come visit her in Chicago
as soon as school let out.

FEBRUARY

Everything has settled back into place with Neil and Katie. Katie became fed up with Neil acting as if they were a couple, and Neil became fed up with Katie only allowing him to touch her when she was drunk. They both complained to me in private, and I did my best to stoke the fires of discontent without making it too obvious. Now we're all friends again, and life feels like it has returned to normal.

"Would you rather be blind or deaf?" Neil asks as the three of us sit in Katie's living room flipping channels on the TV.

Katie smiles. "Deaf. Then I wouldn't have to listen to you. Would you rather be crippled or a dwarf?"

"Crippled, how?" I ask.

"I don't know. Paralyzed from the waist down."

"Dwarf," I say. "They can still have sex. Would you rather be retarded or weigh four hundred pounds?"

"That's stupid," Katie says. "I'd just go on a diet." She shuts off the TV and gives me a wicked smile. "Would you rather shoot a puppy or masturbate in front of your mother?"

"Jesus, Katie," I say, and Neil laughs.

It's a sick game, and deep down we know it, but there is

something undeniably enticing about seeing how far we will go, how low we will sink, before one of us cries mercy.

"We should take the game public," Katie says.

Neil and I laugh.

"I'm serious," she says. "We should put up anonymous signs around school, each one with a different question on it."

"Yeah, right," I say.

"I'm not talking about any of the really bad questions. Just a few of the more harmless ones spread around the school. You know, get people talking about something interesting for a change."

"It would be funny," Neil says. I can see he is starting to embrace the idea.

"Are you both crazy?" I look from one to the other. "Are you both certifiably insane? We could get in serious trouble."

"Nobody would know it was us," Katie says.

"Of course they would!" I yell.

"Whoa, chill the fuck out," Katie says.

"Yeah, how would anyone know?" Neil asks.

"How?" I say incredulously. "I don't know how. But one of us would end up doing something stupid."

"I'll bet you ten dollars we don't get caught," Katie says.

"Oh my God, that is such a bet," I say, sticking out my hand.

This is why my life is so disastrous. If Katie had said to me,

I'll give you ten dollars to help me put up these sick and twisted signs in school, I would have said that ten dollars isn't worth living each day in terror of being exposed. Ten dollars isn't worth overhearing the conversations in the hall about what kind of sick, perverted minds would put up such disgusting signs. Ten dollars isn't worth being called out of class one day with everybody staring and whispering, and being taken to the principal's office and finding my parents already there. Ten dollars isn't worth being put in therapy and listening to my parents blame each other for my problems. But now, because Katie bet me ten dollars, I am making signs and planning strategy of where and when to hang them.

Katie comes up with the first one and insists we tape it up in the boys' bathroom. It says: WOULD YOU RATHER SPEND ONE DAY IN SCHOOL WITH UNCONTROLLABLE GAS OR WITH A PERMANENT ERECTION? The second one we tape outside the cafeteria. It says: WOULD YOU RATHER EAT A FULL PLATE OF YOUR BEST FRIEND'S BOOGERS OR DRINK A FULL GLASS OF A CHAINSMOKER'S SPIT? The third one we tape across from the main bank of lockers. It says: WOULD YOU RATHER SPEND A WEEK IN JAIL OR FRENCH-KISS YOUR GRANDMOTHER? On the bottom of each poster, we write: THE WORST-CASE SCENARIO GAME: FUN FOR THE WHOLE FAMILY.

The next day, the school is abuzz. The posters have been discovered and taken down, but not before enough students have seen one or more of them and spread the word. At lunch, everybody seems to be talking about it, and at one table we see students picking their noses and spitting into glasses.

"This is so awesome," Neil says to me between classes. "I can't wait to put up some more."

"We've got to be careful," I say. "Now they'll be on the lookout."

We decide to lie low for a day or two, though it takes tremendous self-restraint. Katie, in particular, is itching to put up more signs, and I realize that I have never seen her so enthusiastic about anything before.

"This is so fucking awesome," she says as we stand by the lockers after school. "Next time we've got to figure out a way to put up posters that won't get torn down so quickly."

"Krazy Glue," Neil says.

I shake my head. "You're insane."

"Do you have a better suggestion?" Katie asks.

"Maybe, but it means redesigning our posters." I explain that we might be able to disguise what we are doing if we hide our questions in posters that seem to be about something else. We can put something harmless in big letters across the top so teachers and administrators who walk by will just see a sign for some extracurricular activity or fund-raiser and not even pay attention. I grab a piece of paper and show Neil and Katie what I mean.

BAKE SALE

Student Council is having a bake sale

Friday, February 26

All day in the cafeteria

We are trying to raise money

for a school dance.

Please donate **cookies, doughnuts,**

candy, cupcakes, or other baked goods.

Bring money to buy things.

Would you rather live your whole

life with no candy

or with two fingers missing from

each hand?

SHOW YOUR SCHOOL SPIRIT

"It's brilliant," Neil says, and Katie actually jumps up and gives me a hug.

The next day, several posters announcing a bake sale appear on walls throughout the school. The following posters also appear:

INTERESTED IN STARTING
A BAND?

Serious guitar player seeking

singers and musicians

who are into heavy metal
and classic rock.
If you're into Metallica, Iron Maiden,
Ozzy Osbourne, Led Zeppelin, AC/DC,
Bon Jovi, Aerosmith,
then would you like to get
together to jam?
Would you rather spend your whole life
with no music or drink one liter of
vomit on your birthday every year?
FIRST MEETING FRIDAY, February 26,
AFTER SCHOOL IN THE AUDITORIUM

SCIENCE CLUB MEETING
Thursday, February 25, during lunch
Topic:
Planning this year's science fair
Come share your ideas and help make
this year's science fair the
best ever!
Would you rather watch a kitten be
dissected or watch your parents
having sex?
Members and nonmembers welcome
to attend.
Refreshments will be served.

By the end of the day, the signs have been removed, the principal and assistant principal have visited every classroom trying to find out who is behind it all, and the hallways are buzzing with heated debates on the questions we have posed.

"Your parents, dude. That's so sick."

"Not as sick as seeing a kitten cut up."

"The kitten's already dead."

"How do you know?"

"You never dissect animals when they're still alive."

"Can you believe this?" Neil whispers as we stand by our lockers.

I shake my head. As exciting and incredible and unbelievable as this all is, I am still convinced it will not end well. The investigation that the administration has started has left me rattled.

"Katie wants to get a school directory and start mailing out questions to people we hate."

"She's crazy," I say.

"I'm going over to her house later. You wanna come?"

I shake my head. "I've gotta work on my memoir."

It's actually not such a leap from our game to what I'm writing. Right now I'm working on a story about my mentally unstable grandmother, who made me watch a pornographic movie with her when I was fourteen.

"You want us to send any letters for you?" Neil asks.

I laugh. "No way. I don't want any part of this."

The one person I would have considered is Celeste, but lately she's been acting so friendly toward me that I would almost think she was interested if I didn't know better.

As it turns out, Neil and Katie don't end up sending any letters. What happens instead, Neil tells me on the way to school the next day, is they finish half a bottle of vodka, realize they're too drunk to write, and decide to make out instead.

"So I hear you didn't get to the letters yesterday," I say to Katie at lunch.

She shoots Neil a dirty look.

"That's okay," I say, smiling. "It's much nicer to write love notes anyway."

"Fuck you."

"Ooh," Neil says, "I love the dirty talk," and we both start to laugh.

"Screw both of you." Katie starts to get up, then looks at me. "You owe me ten bucks."

"Why?"

"You think I'm going to play this lame-ass game with you losers anymore?"

"We're done?" I feel so relieved not to have gotten caught that I pull out my wallet and hand over the money without complaint. "Now you can buy Neil flowers," I say.

Katie gives me the finger and walks off.

I don't have much time to be jealous. The next day, Celeste asks if I want to go get a cup of coffee after school. I hate coffee. I have a ton of work to do. I'm low on funds.

"Sure," I say.

We sit in Starbucks, and she says she misses me. She asks me about my memoir, and she tells me how good a writer I am. She touches my arm and smiles.

We go back to her house and sit on the couch. She sits very close to me and holds my hand. I kiss her, and she starts to cry.

"What's the matter?" I ask.

She looks up with tears in her eyes. "I just miss Jordan so much."

And then there is Charlotte. We are sitting together at lunch on the last Friday of the month, and I pull out the chapter of my memoir I have just completed.

"Here's mine," I say.

She looks at the paper on the table but does not take it. "I don't know," she says, a look of uncertainty spreading across her face.

"Trust me," I say. "Whatever you wrote is not more shocking than this."

"I don't even have what I'm working on now. I just have my prologue."

"That's okay." I sit silently and try not to appear too eager, but every inch of me is willing her to hand over the pages she has written. I'm surprised how much I want them. What is it I expect to find?

She reaches into her book bag and pulls out a few typed pages and begins to reread them, as if searching for anything that might prove too incriminating.

"Mr. Parke is the only person who has read this," she says.

I nod.

"I don't want anyone else to see it."

"Okay," I say.

She takes a deep breath and hands me the pages. "I don't want to be here when you read this."

"Okay," I say.

She takes my memoir, gathers her things, and walks away. I watch her go, trying to imagine how she will react when she reads what I have written. I cringe as I remember certain details I have included and wonder for a moment whether I have pushed the limits too far this time.

I look down and read the first sentence of her memoir. My breath catches, and I read it again. Then I put the memoir in my bag. I need to be alone in my room before I read any more.

THE TIME I WATCHED A PORNOGRAPHIC MOVIE WITH MY MENTALLY UNSTABLE GRANDMOTHER

The airplane hit a patch of turbulence, and
I gripped the sides of my seat so tightly
that my knuckles turned white. Something so
big and heavy could not possibly stay thirty-
five thousand feet above the ground. The
engines were malfunctioning. The ground
mechanics had not done a thorough check. The
pilot was losing control. The plane was
leaking fuel. I was going to die.

"Are you okay?" the passenger next to me
asked. She was an older woman, perhaps in
her sixties, and she was filled with
motherly concern.

"Why is the plane shaking?" I asked
through clenched teeth.

"It's just a little turbulence," she
said. "Don't worry, dear."

It was incredible that she could be so calm, and not just her, but everyone else on the plane. There they were, reading their books, watching the in-flight movie, sleeping, none of them seeming the least bit worried that we were all about to crash and burn.

"Are you flying by yourself?" she asked.

I nodded. "What's that whooshing sound? Somebody better tell the pilot."

She put a hand on my arm. "Those are just normal airplane sounds. Believe me, I've flown hundreds of times."

"I'm calling the stewardess," I said, pressing the button on the side of my seat.

"It's okay," the woman said reassuringly. She reached into her purse and took out a bottle of pills. "Would you like one of these? It will help you relax."

I took the bottle and examined the label. "You're offering me Valium? I'm fourteen years old."

"Can I have one?" asked the passenger on the other side of her.

"Where's the stewardess?" I said, pushing the CALL button again.

She came reluctantly up the aisle, an impatient look in her eye. "You can't keep pressing the CALL button," she said, "unless you really need something."

"It's raining in Chicago," I said. "How is the pilot going to be able to land?"

The stewardess looked exasperated but managed to keep her voice calm. "It's not at all dangerous to land in light rain. The pilot's done it hundreds of times."

"What if the rain picks up? What if lightning hits the wing? What if the runway is too slippery to land?"

Other passengers were staring at me now, and the woman beside me was trying again to get me to take one of her pills.

"I can't breathe," I said, gulping for air. "There's no air in here."

The stewardess released my oxygen mask and placed it over my mouth and nose. "Breathe," she said. "Just breathe normally."

She had a hand on my shoulder, and as my breathing returned to normal, I felt myself becoming slightly aroused. I closed my eyes and imagined her hand massaging me. As much as I hated airplanes, several of my more erotic fantasies involved stewardesses or other women in uniform.

When I came to, she was no longer there, but the Valium lady was staring at my crotch with a smile on her face.

"My, my," she said. "I'd like a pill that could do that."

For the fiftieth time since we had taken off, I cursed my parents for putting me on an airplane. Even if by some miracle we did not crash, I was now at the mercy of an oversexed, drug-addicted senior citizen. Old people, even normal ones, made me nervous.

My grandmother was not old, she was ancient, and she was certainly not normal. I knew this because every few months my mother would fly to Chicago when my grandmother had stopped taking her medication, was wreaking havoc in her building, and needed to be hospitalized again. According to my mom, my grandmother had been hospitalized for mental illness seventeen times over the past forty years.

"But don't worry," my mom said as she

pushed me toward the airplane. "There hasn't been a major incident in almost a year."

This was of little comfort. I still had vivid memories of those times when she called our house fifteen times each day screaming about murder conspiracies, accusing my father of sleeping with every woman in town, and branding me the leader of a vicious road gang.

This visit was the first I had made alone, and it was hard to imagine how we were going to fill four days together. As it turned out, my grandmother had already planned my entire stay, most of which involved sitting on her couch doing absolutely nothing and watching her doze off. Three times each day we would go downstairs, where they served tasteless, no-salt meals, and my grandmother would show me off to the other old people, who would smile and tell me that my grandmother was a real character.

My grandmother did not often leave her building, but one of her great pleasures was to go to the movies once a week. I knew she was quite a film buff because on the phone she was always recommending movies to me, and her taste in films, much like her personality, was wildly unpredictable. She was particularly excited about a new movie she had recently seen and that she wanted to see again with me. She told me the movie's title shortly after I arrived.

"W-what?" I stammered.

She repeated the title. "Do you know about this movie?"

There had to be some mistake. My grandmother was a senile old woman who was mixing up movie titles. The movie she wanted probably had a similar name. Maybe this could even be an old movie with the same name. "I'm not sure," I said. "What's it about?"

And as she spoke, I realized it was true. My mentally unstable eighty-five-year-old grandmother was planning to take me, her highly impressionable fourteen-year-old grandson, to a pornographic movie.

I knew about the movie because it was about the life of a music star who had made her reputation by wrapping herself around furniture, writhing on the floor, and

licking the bare chests of overly muscular
men in her music videos. The movie featured
the star herself, completely uncensored for
the first time.

We took a taxi to the theater, and my
grandmother tried to prepare me for what we
were about to see. She told me that there
were scenes in the movie that might make me
uncomfortable, but that sex and nudity were
natural, and that this was art, not
pornography. I wanted to assure her that sex
and nudity would not make me uncomfortable
at all. Sex and nudity would make me
excited, aroused, stimulated, and downright
giddy. What would make me uncomfortable was
that I would be watching this sex and nudity
with my eighty-five-year-old grandmother
sitting beside me.

At the theater, the woman selling tickets
asked my grandmother if she knew what the
film was about. I saw people in line
pointing and whispering, and at that moment
I would have sworn off sex and nudity
forever if I could have just been back home,
with my mentally unstable grandmother very
far away. The stares and whispers continued

as we entered the theater, and I imagined
that every conversation in the room was
about us. Then the lights went down and the
movie began.

Those of you who have seen the film can
imagine the next two hours of my life. For
those of you who have not seen the film,
picture this: the music star, scantily
dressed, wraps her mouth around a wine
bottle and pushes it gently in and out,
letting it disappear a bit deeper each time.
She lies on the bed, and as she continues to
swallow the wine bottle, she begins to rub
herself all over with her free hand. The
camera pans back and we realize there is a
fully dressed man in the room sitting in
a chair and watching her. As the man
watches the woman on-screen, my grandmother
watches me.

The whole thing was awful. I tried to
look as natural as possible, but it was
impossible to relax with her studying me.
I looked over at her and pointed to the
screen. The movie's up there, you old hag!
I screamed in my head. She smiled and
continued to watch me. On-screen the man was

beginning to lick the woman's body. I contemplated walking quickly from the theater and hurling myself in front of the oncoming traffic, but realized that my fantastically erect penis would make movement difficult. Yes, that's right. Even though my grandmother was sitting beside me, my independent-minded genitalia had decided to carry on business as usual.

Somehow, I survived the movie. And I must have survived the rest of our visit, though I don't remember what else we did, except sit on the couch and eat tasteless, low-salt meals.

MARCH

My mother committed suicide on my
twelfth birthday. By that time I had
grown accustomed to her bouts of
depression and understood that
sometimes Mommy was just too sad to get
out of bed. On these days, my father
would tell us we had to be extra quiet,
and then he would go out and not come
home until very late. My brother and I
would sit in front of the television
with the volume turned down low, and
when we got hungry I would look for
food in the refrigerator or the pantry
for us to eat.

When I came home from school that
day, I did not even realize at first
that anything was wrong. I deposited
my brother in front of the television
and fixed him a snack. Because it was
my birthday and because Mommy had

promised me a party when I came home, I knocked on her door and crept into her room. She looked like she was sleeping, and I remember thinking how sad it was that she was sleeping on my birthday.

I tiptoed to her bed and looked at her. She was lying on top of her covers, wearing the fancy black dress she sometimes wore to church. At least she had remembered to dress up.

"Mom," I said.

She did not answer.

I shook her gently. "Mom."

Why wasn't she moving? I looked around and saw two empty pill bottles on the floor.

"Mom, wake up," I said, shaking her harder, and still she did not budge.

I started to cry and call her name over and over. My brother, frightened, rushed in and saw me, and the sight of me crying and screaming made him start to cry.

We stood there, holding each other and sobbing. When my father came home

several hours later, he found us
curled up in bed beside her, tear-
emptied and asleep.

My mother's death is the axis around
which the story of my life revolves.
Everything that came before prefigured
this devastating event; everything that
has come since has been an inescapable
consequence. All this I understand
now, though the understanding provides
little comfort. It does not stop my
brother from lashing out against the
world, or my father from trying to
escape it. It does not pay our rent or
make it any easier to spend nights in
the city's family shelter. And it does
not allow me to live the life of a
normal teenage girl or give me the
space I need to figure out who I
really am.
    It feels strange to be telling a story
that is far from over. The best I can do
is to play my part and hope that fate and
time have written me a happier ending
than the one they wrote my mother.

"I don't know what to say," I say to Charlotte when I give her back her memoir. It is Monday, and we are sitting in the cafeteria at the same table where we exchanged our writing three days earlier. She has already given me back mine with comments written all over the pages.

"You're not gonna freak out on me, are you?" she asks.

I manage a smile. "I had no idea."

"There's a lot you don't know about me," she says.

We sit there, neither of us saying anything. I want to ask to read more of her memoir, but somehow it seems inappropriate. I look up and our eyes meet.

"What?" she says. "What are you thinking?"

"Nothing." I look around the cafeteria, then back at her. She seems like she is waiting for me to say something, but I have no idea what to say. Just reading the first two pages has bonded me to Charlotte in a way I don't yet understand, but I know that I have been drawn into something that I cannot easily walk away from. "Do you want to go see a movie after school?" I ask her.

The question takes us both by surprise.

"See a movie?" She laughs and shakes her head as if I have proposed something preposterous. "I can't. I have to pick up my brother."

"I could come with you if you want. Maybe we could all see a movie together."

"I don't think so," she says slowly. "My brother doesn't always do so well with new people."

"That's okay," I say. "I just thought you might like the company."

She looks at me suspiciously. "Why?"

"I don't know," I say awkwardly.

"Look," she says, getting up from the table. "I don't need you to feel sorry for me."

I don't know what to say, so I say nothing, but at the end of the day she finds me at my locker, apologizes for getting upset at lunch, and asks if I still want to come with her to pick up her brother.

"Sure," I say, tremendously relieved that she is no longer angry with me. "Where does he go?"

Henry White, it turns out, is a sixth grader at my old middle school, and standing outside waiting for him brings back a rush of memories, most of them better off forgotten. Here is the building where girls first began actively avoiding me. Here is where Ms. Mitchell, with whom I was in love, caught me with a pornographic magazine during math class. Will any of my old teachers come out and recognize me? Will they even remember who I am?

"There he is," Charlotte says.

A skinny boy wearing black jeans, a Sex Pistols T-shirt, and a leather jacket peels away from a group of older boys and walks toward us. His dark brown hair is shaggy and unkempt and falls to his shoulders, and he has the faint outline of a bruise just underneath his left eye. It is all but impossible for an eighty-pound sixth grader to look menacing, but this boy is clearly making an effort.

"Hi, Henry," Charlotte says.

The boy ignores her and gives me a scornful look. "Who are you?"

"I'm Shakespeare," I say. "A friend of your sister's from school."

"What kind of name is that?"

"A really bad one," I say. "You know, I used to go to this school."

"Did it suck as much then as it sucks now?"

"Probably."

We start to walk off, and I ask Henry about things I remember from my middle school days, which teachers are still teaching, whether they are still teaching the same things, and what he thinks about them. Henry is terse in his responses. Everything about the school sucks, he says, except some of the eighth graders who are pretty cool.

"You coming over?" Henry asks when we get to the bus stop. It is hard to tell from his voice whether this is an invitation or a challenge.

"I don't know." I turn to Charlotte. "Where do you live?"

"We just got an apartment in Fairville," Charlotte says. "You don't have to come. It's kind of far."

It is pretty far, and it's a bad part of town. Why do they live there? And how did Charlotte and Henry end up in schools over here? Does she want me to come? I wonder. Will it look bad if I just take off? What else am I going to do?

"I'll come," I say. "If that's okay."

Charlotte looks at Henry, who avoids her stare. "I guess so," she says.

We have to take the Q bus downtown and transfer to the D. The ride ends up taking almost an hour, and Henry listens to his iPod and takes seats on both buses that are far away from us.

"Is it bad that I'm coming over?" I ask.

Charlotte shrugs. "He needs to learn to deal with other people."

We fall into talk about school and about how much work we have and about where we think we will be next year. Charlotte is amazed by how many schools I have applied to. She is in a very different situation and is not at all sure what next year will bring. She imagines she will probably end up taking classes at a community college nearby because she will need to be around to help take care of her brother. She says right now she isn't even sure she will graduate on time.

"How could you not graduate?" I say.

"Ms. Rigby is failing me for missing so much class, and I have incompletes in history and Spanish."

"That woman is evil." I tell Charlotte about Ms. Rigby confiscating my poem on the day before Christmas vacation.

Charlotte laughs. "The poem you showed me? Wow, I wish I had been there."

We get off the bus in front of a large housing project. There is a 24-hour grocery across the street and a take-out Chinese restaurant on the corner. We walk through a small playground to a building in the development set back from the street. The lock on the door is broken, and I follow Henry and Charlotte up two flights of stairs and into an apartment that is small, dark, and sparsely furnished. We enter into a living room with a couch, a table and chairs, a television, and nothing on the walls. To the right is a tiny kitchen, and to the left, a narrow hallway leading to a bathroom and a bedroom with two beds, a dresser, and a closet.

"This is it," Charlotte says after finishing the tour.

I look around the apartment trying to imagine what it would be like to live here. Does Charlotte share the room with her brother? Does their father sleep on the couch? Where does she do her work? How does anyone have any privacy?

Henry has thrown his jacket and bag on the floor and turned on the television.

"Do you have homework?" Charlotte asks.

Henry ignores her and continues to flip channels.

"Henry," she says, stepping in front of the TV.

"I did it already," he says. "Move."

"When did you do it?"

"Move!" he says, more loudly this time.

"You can't fail your classes again this quarter, Henry. They'll hold you back."

"I don't care," he says. He walks to the refrigerator, pulls out a two-liter bottle of soda, and takes a gulp.

"Henry, that's disgusting," Charlotte says. "Use a glass."

Henry ignores her and puts the bottle back to his mouth. When he is finished, he leaves the bottle on the counter, top off, walks into the bedroom, and slams the door.

"Sorry about that," Charlotte says. "He's been having a rough time at school. Do you want something to drink?"

"No thanks," I say, glancing at the soda.

We sit at the table, and Charlotte tells me I am the first person who has come over to the apartment.

"Really? How long have you lived here?"

"About a month. It's not such a good neighborhood, but at least it's our own place."

On top of the television there is a framed picture, and I get up and bring it to the table. "Are these your parents?" I ask, knowing of course that they are.

Charlotte nods. "That was right after they got married. It's the only picture my father kept."

They are young in the picture, standing on the beach in

bathing suits, the woman looking straight ahead and smiling, the man with his arm around her, gazing down at her face as if he can't believe he is holding something so precious so close. How could these people, so young, so happy, so full of love and life, be the same parents that Charlotte has described?

"My mom loved the beach," she says. "She liked to stare at the ocean."

"You look like your dad," I say.

"That's what people say. I don't really see it." She takes the picture and returns it to the top of the television.

"What does he do, your dad?"

"Now he's working as a house painter." She sits back down and looks at me. "He's had a lot of different jobs."

There is a lot in this answer that is unspoken, and though I am curious to know more, I can see that her father is a subject she is not entirely comfortable with.

We sit at the table, neither of us speaking, and I wonder why I am here and whether she is wondering the same thing. The strangeness of the situation unnerves me, and I begin to think that I need to do something to justify my decision to have come.

Before I can figure out what this is, Henry flings open the door of the bedroom, comes out, and grabs his leather jacket off the floor.

"Where are you going?" Charlotte asks.

He ignores her and walks out of the apartment.

"I need to go after him," Charlotte says, getting up.

I grab my jacket and book bag and follow her out. Henry has gotten a bit of a head start, and by the time we get downstairs he has crossed the playground and is turning down the street.

"You should probably just go home," Charlotte says.

"Are you sure?"

She nods. "Here's a bus coming right now."

I hesitate, though inwardly I am relieved.

"Really," Charlotte says. "It will be better if you go."

I feel a little guilty, but I can tell that my being here is probably making the whole situation worse. This is obviously a family issue, and I should not get involved. Coming here was a mistake. I board the bus, and as it pulls away, I see Charlotte walking beside Henry with her arm draped over his shoulder, looking down at him in a pose strikingly similar to the one in the photograph.

The next day, Tuesday, Charlotte apologizes to me, and Wednesday she is not in school. She ends up being out for the rest of the week, and when she comes back the following Monday, she looks worn out and defeated. I don't have a chance to talk to her during math because she is making up a test she missed, and she skips lunch to go to the library to work. I catch her at the end of the day by her locker and ask her if she's been sick.

She shakes her head. "Henry was suspended from school for fighting, and I had to stay home to watch him."

"That shouldn't be your responsibility," I say.

"My father can't miss work, or he'll get fired."

"Can't Henry stay home alone? He's in sixth grade."

She closes her locker and zips her book bag. "He won't stay home, and it's too dangerous for him to be hanging out on the streets where we live."

"But you can't keep missing school. You'll never graduate."

"What am I supposed to do?" She seems to be on the verge of tears.

It seems crazy that Charlotte is in a situation where she can't even come to school. There must be some other way. "Isn't there anyone else who can watch him?" I ask gently.

"Who?" She is clearly agitated. "We don't have any other family here, and we can't afford to pay someone."

"I just feel like this should be your father's responsibility, not yours."

"He does the best he can," she says, looking away.

Listening to her, I realize how easy I have it. I live in a house where the worst thing is having to share a bathroom with my brother; she lives in a tiny apartment in the projects when she's lucky, and in a homeless shelter when she's not. My mom is a little bit crazy; her mom is dead. My dad sometimes drinks too much; her dad is most likely an alcoholic who neglects his children and cannot hold on to a job. My brother makes me feel jealous because he is popular and has a girlfriend; her brother is a juvenile delinquent who prevents her from living her own life because she has to devote all of her energy to watching over him.

"Have you talked to Mr. Basset?" I ask. "He's a good guidance counselor."

She shakes her head and begins to walk off. "Listen, Shakespeare," she says over her shoulder. "I know you mean well, but it's really none of your business."

"I'm sorry, I just thought he could help you."

She spins around. "I don't need any help."

"Okay," I say in the tone I might use if confronted by a snarling dog. "It just seems crazy for you to miss so much school."

"Worry about your own problems!" She rushes off, and I am left standing there feeling angry and rejected.

I arrive home to find my mom and brother yelling at each other, and this perks me up immediately. Anything that is bad for my brother can only be good for me. I listen to what they are yelling about, and I can't believe what I am hearing. My mother is angry because she found a small bag of pot in my brother's room. My brother is angry because she flushed it down the toilet.

"You owe me fifty dollars!" he screams, storming out of the house.

My mother, still red in the face, finds me standing by the door and confronts me. "Did you know about this?"

"I had no idea," I say, and it is absolutely true. Gandhi smokes pot? Since when? How could I not know? I feel anger and resentment bubbling up in me, not so much because he is doing something I think is bad, but because once again I am discovering he is living a life I know nothing about.

When my father comes home, he seems amused by the whole thing, especially my brother's demand for reimbursement. My mother, too, has calmed down and admits that she probably overreacted.

"What are you talking about?" I say. "He had pot in the house. Aren't you gonna ground him?"

"Ground him? When have we ever grounded either of you?" my father asks.

This, I realize, is true, but neither of us, to my mind, has ever committed such a gross offense.

"Are you smoking, too?" my father asks.

"No," I say angrily, though the fact that my brother is doing it has suddenly made me feel as though I'm missing out on something.

My brother, ever the shrewd businessman, knows when to cut his losses. When he comes home, he does not mention the fifty dollars and even apologizes to my mom for yelling at her. My parents tell him it is natural to want to experiment, and look rather sheepish when he asks them if they ever smoked pot.

"It was a different time," my mother says. "And we didn't really enjoy it."

"Speak for yourself," my dad says, draining his scotch. "Best time of my life."

My mother shoots him a dirty look. "The marijuana today is much stronger. You really need to be careful."

"Listen," my father says. "If you're going to experiment, and I'm not encouraging it, I'd rather you do it in the house, where we know you're safe."

Is he serious?

"I'm serious," he says, noticing my look.

My mother looks uneasy. "Don't go talking about this with any of your friends." As worried as she is about us smoking, she is even more worried about the scandal it would cause if people should find out that she is allowing us to do it in our own house.

My brother seems less shocked by these developments than I am. Later, in his room, he tells me he always suspected our parents had smoked when they were younger, and they would be hypocrites if they made a big deal of it now.

"But it's against the law," I say.

"Whatever," he says. "That's probably why they want us to do it in the house—so we don't get arrested."

After my argument with Charlotte, getting high doesn't seem like such a bad idea, but I'm scared to smoke, because I don't know what it will do to me. The few times I've gotten drunk things have ended badly, and somehow this seems even more dangerous. Neither Neil nor Katie smokes, though Katie says she has done it and didn't like how paranoid it made her feel. To someone who is already convinced the world is conspiring against him, this is not reassuring.

"What's it like?" I ask my brother.

"Getting high?" He shrugs. "Kind of like getting drunk, I guess, but more mellow and without the hangover."

"How many times have you done it?"

My brother does a quick mental calculation. "I don't know. Fifty, maybe."

"Fifty!" I feel my eyes bulging. "Aren't you afraid something's gonna happen to you?"

"Like what?" He quotes me statistics, trying to show that pot is actually less dangerous than either nicotine or alcohol. "You should try it," he says. "It might help you chill out."

With Charlotte avoiding me and Neil and Katie now firmly entrenched as a couple, I find myself alone at my locker Friday after school trying to figure out what to do. It seems so pathetic just to go home and watch TV, and I briefly consider looking for my brother and seeing what he and his friends are up to. As I stare into my locker, Lisa Kravitz walks by with Danny Anderson.

"Hey, Shakespeare," she says, pausing.

I close my locker quickly as if there's something incriminating they might see.

"Do you guys know each other?" she asks.

"You're Gandhi's brother, right?" Danny says.

I nod. "You're friends with my brother?"

He smiles. "We've hung out a few times."

This is news to me. I know Gandhi has a lot of friends and is more popular as a sophomore than I am as a senior, but the fact that he is hanging out with twelfth graders, especially someone as cool as Danny, is pretty amazing.

"Hey, we were just going to hang at my house," Danny says. "You want to come over?"

Danny Anderson is inviting me over? What the hell's going on here? "I've kind of got a lot to do," I say lamely.

"Oh, come on," Lisa says. "It will be fun."

I feel my resistance fade. "Okay," I say, looking at my watch. "For a little while, I guess."

Danny smiles at both of us. "Cool. Let's do it."

Danny, it turns out, lives only five blocks from me. Nobody is at his place when we get there, and we head up two flights of stairs to his bedroom, which is unlike anything I have ever seen. He has converted the space in the attic into a kind of hippie bachelor pad. His bed is a futon mattress on the floor, and there is a couch, a TV, a stereo, and a mini-refrigerator like the ones in hotel rooms. Vintage rock posters—the Beatles, Bob Dylan, the Grateful Dead—cover the walls, and two guitars and a bass stand in the corner. Most striking of all, though, is the sheer number of CDs piled everywhere around the room, at least two thousand, but probably many more.

"It's kind of a mess," Danny says. "But my parents never come up here, so it's cool."

"I've never seen anyone with so much music," I say. "You could open a store."

"I know," Lisa says, "that's what I said."

"Have you been here before?" I ask her.

"A few times."

"How about a little reggae?" Danny asks, taking a Bob Marley CD from one of the many stacks on the floor.

"Cool," says Lisa.

He puts in the music, then goes over to his desk drawer and pulls out a small plastic bag and some rolling papers. I watch him roll a joint with a mixture of fascination and anxiety. This is it, I think. I'm going to smoke pot.

When he finishes, he lights it, takes a hit, and offers it to Lisa. Lisa Kravitz smokes pot? She takes a drag and offers me the joint. I try to act natural, but my heart is racing. I put the joint to my lips, inhale, and immediately start to cough.

"You okay?" Danny asks.

I nod and pass him the joint.

We continue to smoke, and I start to get the hang of it. I can't tell if I'm feeling any different, but I'm certainly not hallucinating or freaking out. This is okay, I think. By the time we've finished the joint, I've decided that getting high with Danny and Lisa is probably the coolest thing I've ever done.

"Hey, you guys wanna do some bong hits?" Danny asks. He

goes to his closet and pulls out a long tube-like thing, open on the top, with a little attachment that juts out from the cylinder. From the mini-refrigerator, he takes a bottle of water and pours some into the tube, then takes a bud of marijuana from a different bag and packs it into the tiny bowl that is attached. "This pot is special," he says, offering Lisa the bong.

She takes the lighter, holds the flame over the marijuana, and begins to suck on the top of the tube. Immediately the water begins to bubble, and smoke fills the cylinder. After a few seconds, she pulls the bowl attachment off the tube, and the smoke shoots up into her lungs.

"Jesus," I say as she exhales and begins to cough.

Danny smiles. "Nice," he says. "Shakespeare?"

"You're gonna have to show me how," I say.

Danny looks like he has just won the lottery. He holds the bong lovingly and launches into a detailed explanation of how it works. Then he passes it to me, like a proud father handing down a precious heirloom to his oldest son. I press the tube to my lips and nod to Danny, who lights the lighter and holds it over the bowl. As I inhale, I hear the water begin to bubble and see smoke rise in the cylinder. It reminds me of the way I used to blow bubbles through my straw in my milk when I was younger, except now I am sucking instead of blowing, and now I am breaking the law and probably doing irrevocable damage to my lungs. I pull the bowl-like attachment from the tube, and the smoke floods upward into my mouth.

Have you ever had one of those coughing fits where you're coughing so hard and uncontrollably that you feel like you might spit out a lung? You know, those body-rattling, stomach-heaving, vessel-popping coughs that leave you doubled over begging for mercy? I've had those fits before, and they're nothing compared to what hits me when all that marijuana smoke comes crashing into my throat.

"I'm dying," I gasp, then lunge into another fit of coughs.

"That was huge," Danny says admiringly.

"Oh my God," I say, catching my breath. "That almost killed me."

"Have some water," Lisa says, passing me the bottle.

I sip slowly. What am I doing here, hanging out at Danny Anderson's house with Lisa Kravitz, smoking marijuana? Smoking marijuana? Have I just smoked marijuana? *Marijuana.* What a strange word. *Marijuana.* Ma-ri-jua-na. Marijuana, marijuana, marijuana, marry wanna, marry wanna.

"Dude, are you okay?" Danny asks.

I realize I am taking tiny sips from the bottle in rhythm with my staccato thoughts.

"That was really weird," I say.

Danny takes a bong hit, then asks if either of us wants another.

"I'm good," Lisa says.

I shake my head. "No way."

Danny moves behind Lisa and begins to massage her back.

"Mmm," she says. "That feels good."

What am I doing here? Are they going to start making out in front of me? I try to look everywhere but at them. Could I possibly feel any more awkward or uncomfortable?

"Where's the bathroom?" I ask.

Danny tells me and I head downstairs. This whole situation is surreal. It's a Friday afternoon, and I'm standing in Danny Anderson's bathroom stoned out of my mind while he and Lisa are probably making out upstairs. My head is spinning, and suddenly I begin to feel boxed in. I need to get out of the house, get some fresh air. Maybe I should splash some cold water on myself. I turn on the faucet, lean over, and try to shovel water onto my face. Most of it gets on my shirt. I look in the mirror and try to suck my shirt dry. What am I doing? I'm sucking on my shirt. I'm freaking out. The colored tiles on the wall, yellow and black, four yellow squares surrounding a black square, four yellow squares surrounding a black square, four yellow squares surrounding a black square. Jesus, the water in the sink is still running. How long have I been in this bathroom, anyway? It seems like forever. What's the plan? The plan, plan, Stan, can, Dan, fan, gan, han. Holy shit, I am so stoned. I look in the mirror. My face still looks normal. I have to get out of here.

I make my way upstairs, clomping loudly so they will hear me coming.

"I'm gonna take off," I say, barely managing to make my way over to my book bag.

"You sure?" Danny is sitting on his couch with Lisa's head in his lap.

"I need some fresh air," I say.

"Are you gonna make it home all right?" he asks.

I stagger to the stairs. "I hope so."

"Hold on." Danny walks me downstairs and lets me out, and I set off on the five-block walk home, taking it one block at a time, trying to look normal, but convinced that everyone I pass can tell I am stoned. All I want to do is make it home, go up to my room, close the door, get into bed, and go to sleep. All I want to do is not have to deal with anyone or anything until I feel normal again.

I keep telling myself that if everything turns out okay, I will never smoke pot again. I am almost home. I can see my house. I can picture the way I will come in the front door and head straight for my room. What about food? I'm starving all of a sudden. I'll have to get some food. Nacho Cheese Doritos. Ice cream. Pringles.

I walk in the door, and my mother is on me before I can escape.

"Where have you been?"

"At a friend's house." Forget the food. Get upstairs.

"Do you know what time it is?" She taps her watch. "We're leaving in fifteen minutes."

I spin around. "What are you talking about?"

"Dinner with Aunt Sylvia. Remember?"

"Oh shit," I blurt before I can catch myself.

She allows herself a smile. "Come on, it's not so bad."

Not so bad? This situation is completely catastrophic, even by my standards. There is absolutely no way I am going to be able to sit through a family dinner with my parents and my incredibly annoying aunt without completely freaking out.

I run up to my brother's room and close the door. He is sitting at his desk IM'ing with his friends.

"I'm screwed," I say.

"What's the matter?" he asks without turning around.

"I'm stoned out of my mind."

He stops typing and turns to me with an incredulous look. "Are you serious?"

"I totally forgot Aunt Sylvia was in town."

He starts to laugh. "What are you gonna do?"

I am pacing his room, running my hands through my hair. "You gotta help me."

My brother doesn't say anything for a moment, and then he smiles. "You shouldn't have told me," he says. "Now I'm gonna fuck with you all through dinner."

"What? You better not."

He rubs his hands together. "Oh, this is gonna be sweet."

"You're an asshole," I say.

* * *

Aunt Sylvia is my father's older sister. She does not have her own family, having never married, so she spends a good deal of time annoying my family instead. Dinner with her will be a torturous affair of listening to her boring stories and answering her boring questions and watching her talk with food in her mouth. Between Sylvia and my brother, I realize I am doomed.

We end up eating at a neighborhood Italian restaurant. We are sitting at a round table, with my mother on one side of me and my brother on the other. From the moment we sit down I begin to feel boxed in, and when my aunt Sylvia begins chattering on about her taxi ride from the airport, I have to restrain myself from jumping up and running outside. As Sylvia goes on and on, my mind begins to drift, and suddenly I remember that earlier in the day I was sucking on my shirt in Danny Anderson's bathroom. The memory comes so suddenly and so vividly that I actually let out a burst of laughter.

"What's so funny?" my mother asks.

By the way everyone is staring at me, I realize I have probably yelped at an extremely inappropriate moment.

"Nothing. Sorry."

They stare at me a little longer, and then Sylvia says, "It was the most awful thing I have ever seen."

She is referring to a car accident she has been describing, but at the moment I am feeling so paranoid that I automatically assume she is referring to my rude interruption.

"I'm really sorry," I say. "Sometimes I just laugh without knowing."

Everybody is staring at me strangely, which I interpret to mean that I am not making any sense and need to explain myself more clearly. Unfortunately, I discover that trying to explain something clearly when you're stoned is about as easy as driving a school bus full of screaming children through an obstacle course blindfolded.

Still, I plunge ahead. "Like one time I was with my friends, I mean, they're not exactly my friends . . . well, one of them is, and then it was his older brother and one of his older brother's friends. But they go to the same school—well, now they've graduated, but then we all went to the same school. And we were at the park and the same thing happened."

Blank stares. I am not making sense. I need to do a better job explaining.

"What are you talking about?" my father asks.

I realize my mind has gone blank. "Wait, what was I talking about?"

"You were telling some story about your friends at the park," Sylvia says helpfully.

"Friends at the park?" I try desperately to remember.

"Yeah," my brother says in a superfast voice. "Youandyourfriendsatthepark."

"Shut up," I say, punching him in the arm.

"What's the matter with the two of you?" my father says sternly.

"Nothing," my brother says.

The waitress brings the menus, and I immediately take refuge behind mine.

Next to me, behind his own menu, my brother is whispering so only I can hear.

"Munchies. Munchy munchies."

"Shut up," I hiss.

"Would you like some gnocchi?" he whispers. "Munchy gnocchi?"

I try to ignore him.

"Isn't that a funny word? *Gnocchi*. Gnocchi, gnocchi."

"You're an asshole," I mutter, and angle myself away from him.

I am having a lot of trouble concentrating on the menu and finally decide it will be easiest just to order what I usually get, which is lasagna and a Caesar salad. The problem is I'm stoned, and this is making me feel like I can eat everything on the menu. Would it be strange to order onion rings, too? The thought of biting into an onion ring dipped in ketchup is making me very excited.

"Are you ready, Shakespeare?" I look up and see that the waiter is at the table and that it's my turn to order. Everyone is staring at me.

"Sorry," I say. "I'll have the lasagna and a Caesar salad."

The waiter nods and writes my order.

"And can I have a side order of onion rings?" I say, feeling extremely self-conscious.

Gandhi bursts out laughing.

"Onion rings?" my mother gasps. "With lasagna?"

The waiter stops writing and looks up, waiting to see if I intend to change my order. This whole dinner is going from bad to worse, and we have barely been here ten minutes, though it feels like ten hours.

"Shakespeare, you're not really ordering lasagna and onion rings, are you?" my mother asks.

"Let him order what he wants," my father says.

"It is rather strange," Sylvia says.

"I'll have the gnocchi," my brother says.

We finish ordering, and I beat a hasty retreat to the bathroom to avoid getting embroiled in a table-wide conversation about my eating habits. I stand in the bathroom and look at myself in the mirror and take a few deep breaths. "This sucks," I say out loud, then laugh, then become wholly absorbed in studying different facial expressions I can make. "Stop," I command myself. "Get it together. Just go out, eat dinner, and act normal."

There are moments in life when we are confronted with nightmarish situations, and somehow, from somewhere, we find the strength and courage and resolve to meet these situations head-on and emerge unscathed. As I walk back to the table, I do so with a determination that I can make it through this dinner, that life will return to normal, and that years from now I will be able to look back on this evening with a sense of pride and accomplishment.

I sit down. Everybody at the table is looking at me. "What?" I say, suddenly nervous and on guard.

"Shakespeare, are you stoned?" my mother asks.

The question hits me like a sledgehammer. I sit stunned for a moment by the force of the blow. Then I feel a smile creep across my face. I feel myself begin to nod, and a voice that sounds curiously like my own says, "I'm stoned out of my mind right now."

My brother's jaw drops. Sylvia gasps. My mother seems frozen, completely at a loss for words. My father lets out a little chuckle before he catches himself and tries to look stern.

What can they do? We are out at a restaurant, we have already ordered, and my mother would rather eat shoe polish than cause a scene in public.

"We'll discuss this when we get home," she finally says.

We eat most of the meal in silence, though my brother keeps looking at me with newfound respect. My onion rings and lasagna are delicious, but by the time we leave my high has worn off and I am feeling sluggish and bloated.

Over the weekend, my mother tries to talk to me about what happened at dinner, and my reluctance to go into it convinces her more than ever that I have larger issues I'm not dealing with.

"Are you depressed?" she asks me several times.

"I'm fine, Mom."

"I really think you should see a therapist," she says.

I shake my head. "Would you drop that already?"

"Just go once," she says. "If you hate it, you don't have to go back."

"Why don't you send Gandhi to therapy? He smokes more pot than I do."

"I'd like him to go, too," she says. "But right now we're talking about you."

I'm tired of arguing with my mother. Would it be so bad to go once? I wonder. I mean, there is something appealing about getting to unload all my issues on someone anonymous and seeing how he reacts.

"Who's the therapist?" I ask. "Not yours."

"No," my mother says quickly. "She recommended one of her colleagues."

"You've talked about this with your therapist?" I am not really upset, but I don't want to make this too easy on her.

She gives me a guilty look. "I just think it's important."

My mother knows I will eventually give in, because it is not in my nature to fight. She knows that deep down I am probably not as resistant to therapy as I pretend to be, and that I am fascinated by the fact that I had a therapist when I was four. What she does not know is that I have actually seen a therapist since that time, and though it was only one visit, the experience was one of the few shining moments in my life.

THE TIME I VISITED
A SEX DOCTOR

I was getting near the end of tenth grade, and my hormones were in a state of frenzy.

"Feed us!" they screamed.

I masturbated constantly—seven, eight, nine times a day, even more on weekends. The way chain-smokers smoke, the way alcoholics drink, that's the way I masturbated.

"My hormones are out of control," I told my friend Neil. "I'm masturbating nonstop."

He was sitting on my bed, looking through a box of CDs. "So what, it's normal for a sexually frustrated fifteen-year-old boy to whack off. I did it myself last night." He looked up and smiled in fond recollection.

"Neil, I'm not talking about once or twice a day, here. I'm out of control."

He pulled a CD from the box and studied it. "Well, how often are you doing it?"

I didn't want to tell him the truth,

because the truth seemed so out of the
bounds of normal behavior that I was afraid
even Neil, who was probably the biggest
freak on the planet, might not be able to
handle it.

"Three times a day?" he asked, looking
up.

I shrugged.

"More? How much?"

I did not respond, and his eyes opened
wide.

"Four? Five?" His voice was rising in
volume.

"Would you keep it down," I hissed.

"SIX?"

I didn't like how excited he was
becoming. "A lot, okay?"

He slid off the bed and stood facing me.
"What's the most times you've ever
masturbated in one day?"

"Neil, you're supposed to be helping me,"
I said in an exasperated voice.

He picked up a calculator from my desk.
"More than ten times?"

"Neil!"

"What do you think the world record is?" His voice brimmed with excitement. "You could be famous."

"I doubt they have a world record for whacking off," I said.

"They might." He held up the calculator. "How many times do you think you can do it in a day?"

I could see where this conversation was going and I refused to get sucked in. "Neil, I want to figure out how to masturbate less, not more."

He looked like I had just popped his favorite balloon.

"C'mon, Neil, you're the only person who can help me."

He studied me for a moment and then nodded. "Okay," he said, "let me think."

I watched Neil close his eyes and stand absolutely still for what seemed like a full minute. I was about to ask if he was okay when a smile curled over his face and he opened his eyes.

"A support group," he said.

"What?"

"You know, like Alcoholics Anonymous."

I laughed. "I doubt they have a group like that for people who masturbate too much."

"Well," he said, "I think it's worth looking into."

"What do you want me to do, walk into a group of total strangers and say, 'Hello, my name is Shakespeare Shapiro and it's been three hours since the last time I whacked off'? No way."

Still, that afternoon Neil and I sat in my room with the Yellow Pages. We looked under *M* for masturbation, under *P* for personal satisfaction and perversion, under *S* for self-love, but we couldn't find anything. I was ready to give up when Neil saw an ad under *S* for sexual counseling and therapy.

"Bingo," he said. "Just what you need."

I shook my head. "I don't think this is for people like me."

"Just call the number," he said, handing me his cell phone. "What harm could it do?"

Because I was someone whose entire life had consisted of one catastrophe after another, I had learned to exercise the most extreme caution. If my mother asked me to go to the store, for example, I would prepare myself to be mugged, to get hit by a bus, or to knock over a shelf of condoms with several of my teachers looking on in horror. Clearly, then, I was not going to do something as rash and reckless as calling a number for sexual counseling and therapy.

"If you call, I'll go with you," Neil said.

I shook my head. "No way."

"I'll even make the call for you." Neil reached out for his phone.

I held it away from him. "I'm not going."

"I'll pay for half of it."

Was he serious? "Why are you so excited about this?" I asked suspiciously.

Neil's voice dripped with feeling, like a bad actor delivering his final soliloquy. "I need this, Shakespeare," he said. "The most exciting part of my day is comparing bowel movements with you. Please, can't we go see the sex doctor? Please?"

Dr. Melody Harmony's office was in a large building where many doctors rented office space. If you looked at the lobby directory, everybody was listed alphabetically with what kind of doctor they were next to their name. Dr. Melody Harmony, sexual counseling, was on the second floor, office number 217.

"Here it is," Neil said excitedly.

I felt gas pains in my stomach. I needed to spend about thirty minutes on the toilet. I let out a few small farts.

The waiting room was almost entirely red, with pornographic magazines spread out across the table.

Neil went to the receptionist and came back with a form for me to fill out. Most of it was basic stuff: name, address, Social Security number. Then came a list of questions regarding my sexual history. Was I married? Was I sexually active? How often did I have sex? Did I ever have problems achieving or maintaining an erection? Was I taking any performance-enhancing medication?

"This is crazy," I said to Neil. "I'm getting out of here."

Neil grabbed my arm. "You can't leave now. We'd still have to pay for the appointment. And think of the stories we'll have to tell." He helped me finish filling out the form and brought it back to the receptionist.

A few minutes later, a door opened, and a large woman with a low-cut orange blouse, shiny red fingernails, a lipsticky smile, and gargantuan breasts came out.

"Which one of you is Shakespeare?" she asked, looking at us.

I got up slowly.

She smiled. "Right this way."

"Can he come, too?" I asked.

"Well," she said. "If that's what you want."

Neil jumped up, and Dr. Harmony ushered us into her office and closed the door.

We sat down, and she sat directly in front of us. I tried unsuccessfully to look everywhere except at her cleavage. Neil had his mouth slightly open and seemed to be in some kind of a trance.

Dr. Harmony let out a little laugh. "Come on, boys, we're never going to get anywhere if all you do is sit there staring at my breasts."

We both blushed and looked at the floor.

"Oh, don't be embarrassed," she said.

"It's perfectly natural for boys your age to be fascinated by breasts, especially ones as big as mine. Now just relax and tell me why you're here."

What could I say? I looked over at Neil for support, but he was still staring hard at the ground, trying desperately not to fall under the power of those enormous breasts again.

"Let me help," Dr. Harmony said kindly. She looked over the form we had filled out in the waiting room. "It says here that you've been feeling some things that don't seem normal."

I nodded.

"And have you been feeling those feelings, too?" she asked Neil.

He looked up, startled. "No, of course not. Those are his answers, not mine. I just came with him. I'm fine."

Dr. Harmony laughed. "Come now, there's no reason to be ashamed. We're all friends here." She paused. "What's your name?"

"Neil."

"Don't you ever get those feelings, Neil?"

"Sometimes, but not as much as him," Neil sputtered.

Dr. Harmony looked at us both for a long time. "Have you talked to each other about these feelings?" she asked.

I shrugged. "Kind of, I guess."

Neil looked at me. "But you still haven't told me how often you do it."

"Why are you so damn interested? Don't you think that's a little weird?"

"Not as weird as whacking off ten times a day."

I felt my cheeks beginning to burn. "I don't whack off ten times a day."

"What, nine, then? You said you do it all the time."

"At least I don't keep written records of every time I take a crap."

Neil's mouth hung open for a second, and he looked at me in horror. "Well, at least I don't go to porno movies with my grandmother."

"Slow down, boys," Dr. Harmony said. She was writing furiously. "I want to make sure I get all this."

Her voice snapped us out of it, and we

looked at each other, shamefaced, then dropped our eyes to the floor, mortified by our performance.

"I should probably go," Neil said, standing up.

"Me too," I said.

"Don't be silly," Dr. Harmony said. "We're just starting to make some progress."

All I wanted to do was escape from that office. Every ounce of my being was concentrated on getting to the door. I would have left a little finger behind if it meant getting out more quickly. Neil was two steps ahead of me.

"Sit down," Dr. Harmony commanded.

We sat. I couldn't sink much lower. I stared at her cleavage and imagined curling myself up in a fetal position between those colossal breasts.

"Now," she said. "Let's look at what's happening here. You two are best friends, right?"

We looked at each other and shrugged.

"And now you're starting to realize that maybe the feelings you have for each other go beyond normal friendship."

Our heads snapped up as if jerked by a chain. "WHAT?!"

"It's totally normal for close friends to become confused about their feelings for each other from time to time."

"We're not . . .," I sputtered.

"You think we're . . .," Neil gasped.

"It's okay," she said. "Go ahead and tell each other how you feel."

And as I sat there, absorbing the full meaning of what Dr. Harmony was saying, I felt myself beginning to relax. If it was normal to fall in love with your best friend, then maybe my problems weren't so serious after all.

I turned and looked at him, and he smiled at me and winked. Then he nodded solemnly, closed his eyes, and took a few deep breaths. Quietly, very quietly, without opening his eyes, he said, "I do feel confused sometimes."

Dr. Harmony nodded. "Good, Neil. Very good. What about you, Shakespeare? What do you want to say to Neil?"

I had to muster every ounce of self-control not to burst out laughing. I shrugged and looked at the floor.

Dr. Harmony sat and waited.

"Sometimes it hurts," I said.

Dr. Harmony nodded. "Yes. When we hold in our feelings, it just makes us hurt more inside."

"I said we could use Vaseline," Neil said.

I put my hand on his arm. "You know I don't like how it feels."

Dr. Harmony nearly choked on her pen. "I—I didn't realize . . . ," she stuttered.

We both started to laugh, and her face slowly registered comprehension.

"Very funny, boys."

We laughed harder.

She let us laugh ourselves out, and then she looked at her watch. "Well," she said, "I guess that's about all the time we have."

We got up to leave, feeling incredibly smug and self-satisfied. It was a sunny day outside, and as we wandered home, talking and laughing, I thought to myself that life was good, and it was good to be me.

APRIL

My life is a disaster. I hate being me.

Today I see Jane Blumeberg holding hands with Eugene Gruber. Eugene Gruber, for God's sake! Jane is my safety. If nothing else works out, Jane is always supposed to be there. I cannot believe that Eugene Gruber has a girlfriend and I don't.

And it gets worse. My mother has invited the Blumebergs to our house for Passover. So now I have to sit through an entire *seder* with Gandhi and Meredith on one side of me and Jane and the specter of Eugene Gruber on the other.

Plus I started therapy.

"An early birthday present," my mom jokes as I head off sullenly to my first appointment.

"I bet Hitler's mother never made him go to therapy," I say.

My mother is not amused. "Well, maybe she should have."

At my session I tell my therapist everything that is wrong with my life, following up my litany of complaints with a detailed account of my pot-smoking experience.

"It sounds to me," he says after listening to me carry on for close to an hour, "that you like to portray yourself as the victim of crazy parents, unsympathetic peers, and unlucky circumstances, because you are afraid to admit that your unhappiness might be your own doing. Smoking marijuana is just an easy way to avoid dealing with your problems. If you want things to change for you, you have to decide you're ready to start taking responsibility for your own well-being."

I can't believe my parents are paying this guy 150 dollars an hour.

Charlotte and I are back on speaking terms, but she has not shown me any more of her memoir, nor have I asked to see it. She rarely comes to lunch these days, choosing instead to head straight to the library after math to catch up on work. I ask her sometimes how things are going, and she says fine, but in unguarded moments I see her leaning heavily against her locker, or with her head down, asleep, in the library. She is still often late or absent, and I know she is struggling to keep not just herself but her family afloat.

What is most difficult for me to understand is why she is so unwilling to ask for help. I'm sure if she spoke to Mr. Basset, he would be able to connect her with people who help families at risk. She could get counseling for Henry or find a support group for her father. But I know she will get angry and defensive if I try to suggest anything, so I don't bother. If she insists on playing the martyr, then that's her business, not mine.

On a whim, I ask her if she wants to come to our house one

night for Passover. My parents go all out for the two *seders,* inviting more than twenty people each night, and I figure that one extra person won't make much of a difference.

"I'm not Jewish," she says.

"It doesn't matter. We always have lots of non-Jews at our *seders.*"

"*Seders?*" she says. "I don't even know what that is."

I explain that the holiday lasts eight days, but it is the first two nights—the *seders,* they are called—that are really the big deal. I explain that during the *seders,* Jewish families sit around the table and retell the story of the Exodus from Egypt, using a guidebook called a *Haggadah.* "There are all kinds of weird rituals," I say, "but you get to drink a lot of wine and eat a lot of really good food."

Charlotte asks more questions, and it seems as if she is seriously considering my invitation.

"You should come," I say, feeling a little ashamed as I realize my eagerness stems mostly from a desire to have a buffer against any awkwardness with Jane.

"It's so nice of you to ask me," she says at last, "but I think it's just too complicated with how late it goes and how far away I live."

"I'm sure someone could give you a ride," I say. "Or we could call you a taxi."

"Maybe next year," she says.

Next year? Next year we're going to be away at college. Next year I won't have to think about Jane Blumeberg and Eugene Gruber.

"Let me know if you change your mind," I say.

College letters have begun coming in, and the first letter I get is from one of my safety schools, telling me I have been wait-listed.

"Don't worry," my mother says, trying hard not to look worried.

"You didn't really want to go there anyway," my father says.

"That's not the point," I say. "It was a safety school."

"What probably happened," my mother says, "is the school saw how overqualified you were and wait-listed you because they know you are just using them as a safety."

If my mother was the guidance counselor at my high school, I think I would shoot myself.

"It's their loss," my dad says, and goes off to fix himself a drink.

Over the next week Yale, Harvard, Columbia, Wesleyan, Amherst, Dartmouth, and the University of Pennsylvania all reject me, but other schools that I was not so sure about— Hamilton, Brandeis, Tufts, Middlebury—offer me spots. I get into all my other safeties, and when all is said and done, eleven schools have accepted me, and four more have placed me on the waiting list, including Brown. The biggest surprise is getting into Vassar, which is one of the best schools I applied to.

"What kind of name is Vassar?" Neil asks me. He and Katie have taken me out for a birthday dinner at Ernie's Pizzeria, because Passover starts so late this year. "It sounds like a combination of *vagina* and *ass*."

Katie, who before dinner downed four shots of vodka at her house, laughs out loud. "That's funny," she says.

"I can't wait to go to college," Neil says. "At Bard you can invent your own major."

"I doubt you can major in bowel movements," I say.

"Ha," says Katie. "That's funny."

For her part, Katie only applied to schools on the West Coast and is going to the University of San Diego. "As far away as I can get" was her main criterion for choosing.

I take another slice of pizza. Starting tomorrow, I'll be relegated to matzo.

The next night, at the first *seder,* I start drinking as soon as we sit down. It is customary to finish four glasses of wine, spread out at intervals throughout the night, but I have decided that tonight I will drink considerably more. Our *seders* tend to be raucous affairs, so no one will pay attention. Many of the people at the table will be drunk by the time the evening is over.

Over the years we've added some twists to the traditional *seder,* one of which is *Haggadah Jeopardy!* At any point during the *seder,* guests can jump in to pose a *Jeopardy!* answer to the assembled group, and everybody tries to come up with the correct question.

We are barely five minutes in when Gandhi begins to hum the *Jeopardy!* theme song. Everybody who has been to our *seders* before laughs and joins in, and when the song is over, he announces the category.

"The category," he says, "is divine miracles. This modern-day miracle is today's equivalent of God's parting of the Red Sea."

"What is the leopard-skin thong?" Harvey Lessing calls out. Harvey is a forty-five-year-old bachelor who has been coming to our *seders* for years and who can always be counted on to be completely inappropriate, even by our standards.

"What is a *seder* that lasts under four hours?" I say, looking pointedly at my father, who has a tendency to ramble on about the meaning of the holiday.

"What is a dutiful and obedient son?" my father counters.

"All good questions," my brother says, "but what I was looking for was, what is the slicing of the brisket?"

Everybody laughs, and the evening proceeds, with people taking turns reading from the *Haggadah,* singing Passover songs, making stupid jokes, and drinking a lot of alcohol. I realize how much fun it would be to share all this with Charlotte and wish suddenly that I had pressed harder for her to come. I look across to Jane. She is drinking juice, even though we are all allowed to drink wine. Our eyes meet, and she smiles. Now that she is unavailable, she is far more desirable than she ever has been in the past. Her face is so soft, her eyes so big and innocent. She has silky hair that falls all the way down her back, and small breasts that poke out from behind her white blouse. I pour myself another glass of wine.

"I heard you're going to Vassar next year," she says. "That's one of the schools I want to apply to."

"I was surprised I got in."

"Are you excited to graduate?"

I shrug. "I guess so."

We don't talk to each other for a while after that, and I drink some more wine. The more I drink and the more I look at her, the more preposterous it seems that she is going out with Eugene Gruber, and I begin to convince myself that she is only going out with him because she thinks I am not interested.

My brother has been watching me watch Jane, and when Meredith and Jane go off together into the kitchen, he leans over and tells me I should ask her out.

"What are you talking about?" I say.

"Jane. She likes you."

I feel my heart leap. "Isn't she going out with someone?" I ask.

"Who? Eugene Gruber? They're just friends now. She told Meredith she wants you to ask her to the prom."

The girls come back to the table, whispering and giggling, and I pour myself another glass of wine. Is Jane really waiting for me to ask her to the prom? How am I supposed to do it in a room with twenty other people, including her parents? I drink some more wine and plan my strategy. The bathroom is on the second floor. At some point before the end of the evening Jane will have to go. When I see her get up I will follow her upstairs, and when she comes out of the bathroom I will ask her. I finish my glass and pour another.

Gandhi begins to hum the *Jeopardy!* theme song again. "The category," he says, "is holy numbers."

Everyone smiles.

"The answer is sixty-nine."

I nearly spit my wine out, and it goes up my nose.

"Now we're talking," Harvey says.

"No X-rated questions," my mother warns. My brother looks temporarily confused, and then starts to laugh.

"I don't get it," Jane says to me.

"It's stupid," I say.

"How many bottles of wine will we finish tonight?" my father calls out.

Everybody laughs, and my brother shakes his head.

"When's the last time the Mets won the World Series?" someone says.

People take a few more guesses, and then everyone gives up.

"The correct question is, on what page do we get to eat the festive meal?" he says.

"Festive meal, indeed," Harvey Lessing says with a smirk.

My mother gives him an annoyed look.

The first half of the *seder* finally ends, and we begin to eat. I pile my plate high and shovel food into my mouth. Jane, I notice, eats only half her bowl of soup and picks daintily at a piece of brisket. At least she's not a vegetarian.

The meal lasts over two hours, and I begin to wonder whether Jane will ever go to the bathroom and what I will do if she doesn't. I'm feeling pretty light-headed by this point, and I'm starting to imagine scenarios in which I lead her back into the bathroom when she emerges, I close the door behind us, and we begin to make out. I realize, with a start, that I have an erection, and it's at this moment that Jane gets up quietly and leaves the room.

I've had too much wine to be able to make a new plan, so I wait several seconds, then get up, walk upstairs, and hover outside the bathroom door. My heart is pounding, and I realize that I have had a lot to drink, because this is not something I would ever do sober and certainly not sober with an erection. It's the weirdest thing just standing there, and I pray that nobody else comes upstairs and sees me. I look down at my pants and see they are still pushed out at the crotch. This is crazy, I think. What am I doing? Just turn around and go back downstairs.

The toilet flushes, I hear the sink run, there is a moment of silence, and then Jane opens the door.

"Oh," she says, blushing. "I didn't know you were waiting." She steps past me, and I realize the moment is about to pass.

"Jane," I say, and she stops and turns.

We stand there for a second, and I forget what it is I am supposed to be doing. I take a step toward her, put my hand on her shoulder, and lean forward to kiss her.

She turns her face so I end up kissing her cheek, then backs up two steps.

"I'm going to go downstairs," she says quietly, and hurries off.

I stand there for a moment. Then I go into the bathroom and shut the door. "Idiot," I hiss at myself in the mirror. "What were you thinking?"

I realize I have to go back downstairs and sit across from Jane for the rest of the evening. I doubt she will have told anyone what I did, but how will she act toward me? Should I apologize? What if she acts like nothing happened? Will she still want to go to the prom with me? Did she notice I had an erection?

By the time I get downstairs, the final part of the *seder* has begun. Jane looks up briefly from her *Haggadah* and gives me a tight smile before looking back down. She does not make eye contact with me for the rest of the night.

When the *seder* ends, there is a little milling about, and by

11:30 people are starting to say good night. I say good-bye to our guests as they leave and tell Jane I'll see her in school.

That night I dream I am at an appointment with my therapist, except my therapist is Jane Blumeberg's father.

"I asked Jane to the prom," I tell him.

He nods. "How did it feel to ask her?"

"I don't know. I was a little nervous, I guess. It's hard to ask a girl out. You never know what she's gonna say."

"But you did it anyway. That takes courage."

"I guess. It made it easier that I was a little drunk."

"Well," he says, smiling. "There's no question that alcohol can break down some of our inhibitions."

I sit quietly for a moment, wondering how much I should confess. "I did something stupid, though," I say at last. "After I asked her, I tried to kiss her."

His eyes open a bit wider at this. "Why do you suppose you did that?"

"I was kind of drunk."

"It's easy to use alcohol as an excuse. Did you want to kiss her?"

I look away. "I don't know. I guess so."

He waits until I look back at him. "How did she react?"

"She sort of turned away."

He nods. "How did that make you feel?"

"I don't know. Like an idiot, I guess."

We are silent, and it seems like he is waiting for me to say more.

"Are you nervous about taking her to the prom?" he finally asks.

"I'm not really nervous. I just don't know what's going to happen. I can't really tell if we're going as friends, or if we're going as a couple."

"What do you think?"

"I don't know," I say. "She seemed happy that I asked her, but she kind of freaked out when I tried to kiss her."

"Turning away doesn't sound like freaking out. Maybe she was just surprised."

"Maybe. It's kind of weird having this conversation with you."

He smiles in a way that seems intended to convey complete understanding. "Listen, Shakespeare," he says gently. "This is my job, and you're my patient. You should feel free to talk about anything you want."

We sit there for a while, not saying anything.

"What are you thinking?" he asks.

"I always imagined making out with my prom date in the back of a limo."

His eyes narrow a bit, and he presses his lips together.

I feel myself gaining momentum. "I mean, if you can't get your date to make out with you at the prom, it sort of seems like a waste to go through all the trouble of renting a tux and a limo and paying all that money to go."

"It sounds like you're less interested in going to the prom than in finding a girl who will make out with you, as you put it."

"That's true," I say.

He taps his pencil on his desk. "Do you think Jane is aware of how you feel?"

"What, I'm supposed to tell her?"

"It seems to me that you would want to make sure that you both feel the same way. Especially if just going is as much trouble as you say."

"What, I'm just supposed to go to Jane and ask her if she'll make out with me on prom night?" I laugh and roll my eyes. "I can't do that."

"What do you think you should do?"

"I don't know. Maybe we just shouldn't go."

He raises his eyebrows but does not say anything.

"The whole thing just seems like such a hassle," I say.

"Did you think about all this when you decided to ask her in the first place?" It seems there is a slight edge to his voice.

"I only asked her because my brother said she wanted to go with me."

"You think this is your brother's fault?"

"It's true. I had a whole list of girls I was interested in. Jane was one of my safeties."

His eyes open wide. "Your safeties?"

"Like with colleges. You apply to a few safety schools just in case you don't get into any of the others."

He considers this for a moment. "I see." He looks at me, and I can tell he's trying to make up his mind about something. "Shakespeare," he says at last, "I'm going to talk to you for a minute, not as a therapist but as a father. I was happy when I heard you had asked Jane to the prom, because I saw that she was happy. But after this conversation, I have serious reservations about allowing her to go with you."

"I understand," I say a bit too quickly.

He holds up his hand. "Let me finish. I know that if I tell Jane she cannot go, I will also have to tell her why, and it would be devastating for her. I also know that if you try to back out, you will end up making things even worse. Since you've already asked her and she's excited to go, you will take Jane to the prom, you will treat her with the respect and the dignity she deserves, and if I find out that you have hurt her in any way, I will exact a terrible vengeance, the likes of which you can only imagine." He pauses and fixes me with his gaze. "Is all that clear enough for you?"

I work hard to avoid Jane in school after that, especially when I see from a distance that she and Eugene Gruber are indeed still a couple. I am furious with my brother for setting me up. I am furious with my parents for inviting the Blumebergs to our house in the first place. And I am furious with myself for getting so drunk and acting like a complete idiot.

Then again, getting drunk and acting like a complete idiot does run in the family. I know my parents both drank a lot before I was born, and some of the more disturbing stories they've told me about the origin of my name must have involved a considerable amount of alcohol consumption. They say they have cut back—which does make me wonder about the health of my father's liver—but they still drink too much on occasion, and my father, in particular, has turned in a few staggering performances. I'm not saying that getting drunk and acting like a complete idiot is genetic, but I will say that my father has not always modeled appropriate behavior in my presence. And if I were to point to a single defining experience of questionable father-son bonding, it would have to be that summer night in Rome when I was sixteen.

THE TIME I SAW MY FATHER GET DRUNK AND ACT LIKE A COMPLETE IDIOT

I took a Valium and tried to relax. How my parents had gotten me on an airplane again was beyond me, but here I was, about to embark on a seven-hour flight thirty-five thousand feet above a shark-infested ocean.

My parents had insisted that I take the Valium and even suggested I take two. If they were going to be on an airplane with me, they wanted to make sure I was as relaxed as possible.

It was the summer after tenth grade, and we were on our way to Italy for a family vacation. Twenty years earlier my parents had spent their honeymoon in Venice, Florence, and Rome, and they were returning now for the first time to these cities that held such magical memories for them.

The thing about my parents is that neither of them can remember anything. My father speaks about the past with great conviction and authority, but according to my mother, everything he says is a fiction he has invented over the years that bears little semblance to what actually happened.

"Wait till you see Venice," he said. "Your mother and I got so lost there on our honeymoon, we ended up walking around the city all night."

I looked at my mother, and she shook her head.

"Your mother doesn't remember anything," my dad said.

I had mixed feelings about this trip. On the one hand, I was excited to see Italy and to stay in Italian hotels and to eat at Italian restaurants and to stare at Italian women. On the other hand, I was dreading spending two weeks alone with my family. My father would be taking us on forced marches through each city, my mother would be worrying all the time that we looked like tourists, and I would have to share a room with Gandhi, which would mean no privacy to masturbate, except in the bathroom.

For the most part the trip ended up being about what I expected. Without going into all the lurid details, here are some of the highlights:

1. We ordered calves' liver our first night in Venice because my mother forgot her dictionary and was too embarrassed to ask for an English menu.
2. A pigeon shat on me in Piazza San Marco.
3. We stood in the pouring rain outside a museum in Florence to see Michelangelo's *David*, which is a statue of a naked man with an uncircumcised penis.
4. My father nearly got us killed driving on the Autostrada between Florence and Rome because he kept looking at the map, even though all he had to do was stay on the same highway the whole time.

5. My brother put on a *yarmulke* as we
   walked through the Vatican, and
   asked our guide whether the Pope
   had any Jewish friends.
6. My parents spent a lot of time
   reminiscing about their honeymoon
   and showed up at breakfast each
   morning with smiles on their faces.
7. I became constipated.

What really makes this story worth
telling, though, is the night we spent with
Robert in Rome.

Robert Sweeney had been a classmate of my
father's in graduate school. According to my
mother, he was the kind of friend you are
supposed to outgrow by the time you are
ready to settle down and have a family. Both
he and my father liked to drink, and when
the two of them got together, they always
managed to achieve staggering levels of
intoxication. I had only met Robert a couple
of times; after I was born, my mother had
pushed my father to reform some of his ways,
and that meant much less contact with his
old friend.

We ran into Robert, quite by chance, the day before we were supposed to return to the States. I remember walking down the street and suddenly hearing a booming voice that made everyone around stop and stare.

"SHAPIRO!"

We all turned and saw a small, round man who looked like a troll.

"Sweeney, you old rascal," my father said, smiling broadly.

"Oh shit," I heard my mother mutter.

Robert was living in Rome for the year, on sabbatical. He and his third wife had recently been divorced, and he had decided that a change of scenery would be good for him.

"We'll all have dinner together," he said. "My treat. Are you boys drinking?"

My father laughed. "Don't corrupt them yet."

"Remember we're leaving early tomorrow," my mother said, and I detected a note of despair in her voice.

"Don't worry," Robert said. "I'll make sure he behaves."

My father and Robert made the

arrangements, and we met later that night at a large, popular restaurant, which was still relatively empty at 8:00.

"A toast," Robert said as we all held up our drinks—Cokes for Gandhi and me, a glass of wine for my mother, and scotch for the two men. "To many more happy reunions."

I had watched my dad drink my entire life, so at first I paid little attention to the amount of alcohol he was consuming. It was only toward the end of the meal, when he began banging on his water glass with his spoon, that I realized he was more drunk than usual.

"Hey, boys," Robert said. "Try this." He stuck the prongs of his fork up his nostrils.

I smiled and thought to myself what an idiot this guy was.

"Cool," Gandhi said, and imitated Robert.

"Stop it," my mother said. "You're making a scene."

In fact, nobody was paying us the least bit of attention. It was after 10:00 by this point, and the restaurant had become crowded and boisterous. This was a good thing because my father and Robert were just getting warmed up.

"A toast," my father sang out, pouring what must have been his tenth glass of wine. "To fucking Italy."

"Fucking Italy," Robert said, and they smashed their glasses together, shattering both of them.

Robert pulled his chair to the table next to ours and looked around, wild-eyed. "Does anybody have an extra glass? All I need is one glass. Two glasses, I need. Hey, are you using your glass? What's the matter, you don't speak English? Glass. The thing you drink out of."

"Don't you think you've had enough?" my mother hissed at my father.

My father brandished his spoon. "Never!" he yelled.

I didn't know whether to laugh or cry, but when the restaurant manager came over and asked if there was a problem, I wanted to hide under the table.

"They're just drunk," my brother said. Why wasn't he as embarrassed as I was?

"DRUNK?" Robert shouted, wheeling back to our table. "WHO'S DRUNK?"

"*Il conto, per favore,*" my mother said, miming writing a check to the manager. "I'm so sorry."

"What are you sorry about?" my father slurred. "You don't have to apologize for me. I'm going to take a leak. Come on, Robert."

The two of them staggered away, and my mother said she was sorry we had to see this.

"It's funny," my brother said.

I shook my head. "No, it's not. It's sad."

"Well," my mother said. "If I divorce your father, you'll understand why."

She must have seen the stricken look on my face. "I'm just kidding," she said. "Listen, if your father insists on staying out with his friend, I want you to go with them. If you're along, at least they won't try to pick up women."

"Why don't you go?" I asked.

My mother shuddered. "I can't stand the two of them together. Besides, I need to go back to the hotel and finish packing."

"I don't want to go out with them," I said. "We'll probably end up in jail."

"I'll go," my brother said.

My mother shook her head. "You're coming back to the hotel with me. You'd probably just encourage them."

And that was how I came to spend my last night in Italy in the company of two extremely drunk grown men.

My biggest concern was that they would lose me. I had no desire to be deserted in a foreign country in the middle of the night. I shouldn't have worried. My father and Robert were so loud I was sure I would be able to hear them even if we got separated.

"How old are you, Shakespeare?" Robert asked as we wandered the narrow alleys of Campo de'Fiori.

"Sixteen."

He burped loudly. "When I was sixteen, I was a real asshole."

You're still an asshole, I thought.

"Do you have a girlfriend?"

I felt myself blush. "Nah." I shook my head.

"Good. Girls are nothing but trouble. You know, your father used to be a real womanizer."

I did not want to hear this.

"Before he met your mother, he used to—"

"Robert," my father slurred. "There are children present."

Robert looked at me and smiled, then began to gyrate back and forth. "Bang, bang, bang, bang, bang."

Please, Lord, I thought. Just take me now.

"You know what we should do?" Robert said.

A feeling of dread enveloped me. "What?"

"Get some more drinks, then go jump in the Trevi Fountain."

"That's nowhere near here," I said.

"So? Have you got someplace you need to be?"

As far away from you as possible, I thought.

My father seemed indecisive.

"You're leaving tomorrow," Robert said. "This is your last night."

"It is my last night," my father said, and I could feel him gaining momentum. "What do you think?" he said, looking at me and smiling.

What did I think? I thought my father should act like someone his age and not go running around Rome all night like a drunken teenager. I thought we should say good night to Robert and go back to the hotel before anything worse could happen. I looked at my father and could see that he wanted to go, and the only thing holding him back was a twinge of fatherly concern for my well-being. Why wasn't my brother here instead of me? He would have been happy to go with them, and I could be back at the hotel in bed, watching television. I realized suddenly how pathetic that was. My brother, two years younger, would be reveling in a night like this, and all I was doing was complaining. Here I had an opportunity to be out all night in Rome, and I wanted to be in bed, watching television. No wonder my brother had so many friends and so many girls who seemed to like him. He knew how to embrace life instead of shying away from it. I was sixteen already, and what did I have to show for it?

"I think I need a drink," I said.

"That's my boy," Robert said, clapping me on the shoulder.

"What the hell?" my dad said. "There's no drinking age here anyway."

We sat outdoors at a café on the Piazza Navona, and Robert ordered a bottle of wine. By the second bottle, my father and Robert had moved from a hyperactive state to a philosophical one, and as we sat outside, sipping wine and looking at the Fountain of the Four Rivers, the conversation became downright comical.

"You know what's bullshit?" Robert said.

My father drained his glass. "What?"

"The Bible."

"The Bible's total bullshit," my father agreed.

"Why's the Bible bullshit?" I asked.

Robert turned his attention to me. "Take any story and analyze it. Go ahead, pick a story."

I said the first thing that came to mind. "Noah's ark."

Robert gave a triumphant laugh. "That's about the most obvious piece of bullshit in the whole damn book."

"Two of every species," my father said. "How did Noah keep the lions from eating the zebras when they were on the ark?"

I smiled and took a sip of wine. "Well, what about Abraham?"

"Abraham!" Robert roared. "The guy who knocked his wife up when she was ninety?"

"What about Methuselah?" my dad chimed in. "The Bible says he lived to be nine hundred and sixty-nine."

"Bullshit," Robert said. "All of it."

"You know what else is bullshit?" my father said, pouring himself another glass.

"What?" I asked.

"Water."

"Water?" I said. "What are you talking about?"

My father swirled the wine in his glass and sniffed it. "It's bullshit. I don't drink things that have no taste."

"I'll tell you what's bullshit," I said.

My father looked amused. "What?"

"Everything that's coming out of both of your mouths."

"The boy's on to us," Robert said. "What should we do?"

My father made a slashing motion across his neck. "Kill him and get rid of the body."

I laughed, and my father put his arm around me. "You're a good kid," he slurred.

We finished the wine and began to walk without purpose or direction. I was feeling a bit light-headed, but I was certainly in better shape than either of the adults. We rambled down moonlit streets and alleys, through piazzas that suddenly opened up before us, across a bridge, and then across another.

It was close to 3:00 a.m., and though there were still people out, the city felt like it was winding down and going to sleep.

"Where the hell are we?" my father asked as we walked past yet another church.

Robert looked around. "Beats me. Everything here looks the same."

"You're kidding," I said.

My father lay down on the ground. "I'm just gonna take a little rest here," he said.

I looked down at him sprawled out on the concrete. A young couple passed by and pointed, then walked away laughing. This is my father, I thought. God help me.

At breakfast the next morning, only my mother was smiling.

"Your father has a hangover," she told us cheerily. "That's what happens when a grown man acts like a twenty-one-year-old fraternity boy."

My father managed a sheepish grin and winked at me.

"You're supposed to drink a lot of water before you go to bed," my brother said.

"How are you such an expert?" my mother asked.

"Water is bullshit," I said.

My father started to laugh, then grabbed his head. "Oh," he said. "I feel awful."

We made it to the airport and boarded our flight. The trip home ended up being about what I expected. Without going into all the lurid details, here are some of the highlights:

1. My mother accidentally gave me an estrogen pill instead of a Valium. "Oh my God," she said, "don't take that." I told her I already had, and she started to laugh. "You just took 2.5 milligrams of female hormones." So I spent most of the flight feeling my chest to see if I was growing breasts.

2. My father smelled my Salisbury steak airplane lunch and vomited into his barf bag.

3. I ate my Salisbury steak lunch, felt my constipation begin to give way, and found myself behind five other Salisbury steak victims in line to use the lavatory. We hit a patch of turbulence just before my turn.

4. The in-flight movie was *A Room with a View*, which is a boring British film that features a scene of naked men running around with their penises flapping. It's hard to tell whether or not they're circumcised.

MAY

Even though we don't graduate until the middle of June, the sense of impending freedom has begun to sweep through the ranks of the senior class. Lateness is up, attendance is down, students linger in hallways between classes, talking in clusters and hugging each other. We are by no means done with our work—we have finals in most classes and our memoirs are due at the end of the month—but with everybody into college already, with the warm weather around us, and with the senior prom just ahead, it is hard to worry too much about anything.

I am a nervous wreck. My first problem is that I have no idea how to end my memoir. I wouldn't care so much, except Mr. Parke has been telling me that if I finish strong, I have a good chance of being chosen as a finalist for the writing award at graduation. What happens is that each writing teacher chooses two memoirs from each of his or her classes. Mr. Parke, Ms. Glass, and Ms. McCurry each teach two sections of writing, meaning that out of one hundred and forty-four total memoirs, only twelve are chosen. The twelve final memoirs are sent to a panel of three judges made up of previous winners of the award. Although the twelve finalists know they are finalists, nobody, except the judges, knows who the award recipient will be until graduation. I don't expect to win, certainly not after reading what Charlotte has written, but how sweet would it be if I was chosen and Celeste was not. We've been friendly to each other ever since she cried to me about missing Jordan, but I'm still angry at her for leading me on.

And then there's my other worry. Prom. The ultimate testing ground for the haves and have-nots. When the year started, when I made my list of girls to go along with my list of colleges, it was with prom in mind. When I suffered through *Montezuma's Revenge* with Celeste, I imagined how good I would look with her at my side. When I made a pass at Jane Blumeberg, even though I had ignored her all year, I did so because at least I would have a date. Now Celeste is going with Jordan, and Jane is going with Eugene Gruber. Everybody is going with somebody, except me.

"Why don't you just ask Charlotte?" Neil keeps saying. He is going with Katie and wants me to ask Charlotte so we can all share a limousine.

Of course I have thought about this but come up with a dozen reasons not to. "She wouldn't want to go," I say.

"How do you know?"

"Prom isn't her kind of thing. Plus, it's all so expensive. She can't afford to buy a ticket, a dress, and chip in for a limo."

"Well, why don't you offer to pay for her?" Neil asks.

"I would, but I don't think she would let me."

"Well, it can't hurt to offer."

I keep putting it off, but with Neil hounding me and with prom less than a week away, I finally agree to do it. It feels strange asking Charlotte, because our whole relationship has been so odd and because we are neither a couple nor close friends. What will she think? Will she be surprised? Suspicious? She already turned me down once when I invited her to our house for Passover.

I do it as casually as possible as we walk from math class to the cafeteria. "Hey," I say, as if the thought has just occurred to me. "I was thinking it might be fun to go to the prom. Do you want to go with me?"

"Wow," she says, smiling. "That came out of nowhere. It's this Friday, right?"

"Yeah." I try to seem relaxed, though I'm shaking inside. "Listen, if it's too short notice, I totally understand."

"I'd like to go," she says simply, "but I have to check a few things. Can I tell you tomorrow?"

"Sure," I say, feeling both relief and gratitude. "Listen, if it's an issue of money—"

"No," she says quickly. "It's not that." Her tone has become sharper, and though I am not at all convinced, I know better than to press her.

The next day on our way out of math class she tells me she can go.

"You can?" I say. "That's great. Do you want to share a limousine with Neil and Katie? They've already reserved it."

"That sounds fun," she says, but she has a slightly troubled look.

"Neil's parents are paying for the whole thing," I lie. "It's an early graduation present."

"Are you sure they want to share it?"

"Definitely. They invited us."

She takes a moment to process this, and I make a mental note to talk to Neil and Katie before Charlotte has a chance to thank them. This, I realize, will be extremely difficult if she is coming to lunch right now.

"Do we all meet somewhere first?" she asks.

"I'm sure we can pick you up at your apartment." I am so focused on trying to figure out how I will get to Neil and Katie before Charlotte does that I do not even consider how private Charlotte is about her home life.

"It's out of the way," she says quickly. "It will be easier if I just come to your house first."

This is not a great option, either. There is no telling what my parents might do to embarrass me.

"We'll figure it out," I say.

As we approach the cafeteria, Charlotte stops and turns. "I should go to the library," she says. "I have a ton of work I need to finish in the next few days."

"See you," I say. I enter the cafeteria with a tremendous feeling of relief.

The next day Charlotte is absent, and the day after that, too. Her absence makes me paranoid. Is she sick? Is she avoiding me because she has changed her mind? Has something happened with Henry again that will prevent her from going? I leave lunch early on Thursday, call her house from my cell phone, and discover that her number has been disconnected.

"What should I do?" I ask Neil at the end of the day. "Prom's tomorrow night, and Charlotte's been out the last two days."

"Just buy her a ticket," Neil says. "She can always pay you back."

"What if she doesn't come to school again tomorrow?"

Neil laughs. "Why are you so worried? She said she was gonna go. Just call her."

"I tried. Her phone's disconnected."

"So go by her house."

"It's not so simple," I say, and because I am a nervous wreck and because Neil and I have always shared everything with each other, I tell Neil everything I know about Charlotte, about what I read in her memoir and about what I saw when I visited the apartment and about Charlotte's absences and about the precariousness of her family's existence.

Neil listens to everything I say with an astonished look.

When I finish, he is silent for a moment, and then he says, "Jesus, Shakespeare, that's some heavy shit."

I nod.

"Do you think they got evicted?"

"I don't know what to think."

"Well," he says, "I still think you should go over there and see. I'll go with you if you want."

"I don't know." The whole situation is making me extremely uneasy.

"Look, Shakespeare, if she's there we can iron out our plans for prom. If she's been evicted, don't you think we should be trying to help her?"

So instead of going home that day, we take the long trip to Fairville and get off in front of the huge housing development where Charlotte lives. I expect Neil to show some discomfort in the surroundings, but he is swept up in our adventure and marches alongside me across the playground and to the entrance of Charlotte's building. The lock has been fixed, and we stand outside wondering what to do next.

"I guess we should just wait for someone to come let us in," I say.

We wait a few minutes, and then Neil asks what floor she lives on.

"Third," I say. "Why?"

"Does their window face out to us?" he asks.

"You're not gonna yell up?"

"Why not?"

"Look where we are," I say, sweeping my hand around to display our surroundings. "We'll probably get mugged or something."

"You are so paranoid," Neil says. He tips his head back and yells, "CHARLOTTE!"

"Jesus, Neil," I whisper.

"CHARLOTTE!"

I am about to walk away when a window above us opens and Charlotte looks out. She seems astonished to see us and tells us to wait. Thirty seconds later the door to her building opens and she walks out.

"What are you doing here?" she asks. She is wearing sweatpants, a T-shirt, and flip-flops, and she does not seem happy to see us.

"I tried calling," I say lamely, "but your phone's been disconnected."

She looks at me, then at Neil, then at me again. "What did you want?"

Suddenly the whole trip seems so preposterous I don't know what to say. "You've been absent, you know, and I was getting nervous . . ." I stop because I have no idea how to finish the sentence.

Charlotte's eyes go back to Neil, and he says, "We just

wanted to make sure everything was all right, and that you didn't get evicted."

Charlotte looks at me once more, her mouth turned down, her eyes narrowed. "I'm fine," she says. Then she turns, unlocks the door, and disappears inside.

"Charlotte, wait," I say. I catch the door before it closes, but she continues up the stairs.

"Wait for me," I say to Neil, and I chase after her.

She stops on the second landing and allows me to catch up. There are tears in her eyes, and she brushes them away.

"Charlotte," I say.

"Why did you bring him here? Why are you talking about me with your friends?"

"I'm not. I mean, it's just Neil."

"What did you tell him?"

"I'm sorry, Charlotte, I just got nervous. You weren't in school."

"I'm not in school a lot. So what?"

I stand there, not knowing what to say.

"Just go, Shakespeare," she says angrily.

"What about prom?" I ask.

I see tears forming in her eyes again. "Just go." She turns and hurries up the stairs, and I hear her door open and slam shut.

* * *

At a little past 8:00 on prom night, a limousine pulls up in front of my house, and Neil and Katie—he in a tuxedo, she in a black dress and combat boots—drag me off the couch, order me upstairs to change, and, ignoring my protests, lead me into the limo and make me take a drink of vodka from Katie's flask. The two of them are already well on their way to getting hammered, and I decide that if I'm going to be miserable all night, I might as well be miserable getting drunk with my two best friends. I take another drink and smile at Neil, who is watching me and beaming.

"Pace yourself," he says. "We've got this limo rented all night."

Outside the banquet hall where the prom is being held, limos are lined up, couples are milling about in the parking lot, and everybody seems to be in a festive mood. I see Danny Anderson walking by with a few friends, and when he sees me he motions me over.

"We're going to smoke a joint, you wanna come?"

"No thanks," I say. "I'm good." This whole scene is too much to deal with as is. Last thing I need is to get high again.

I follow Neil and Katie inside, smiling, waving, saying hi to people I never talk to, pretending I am happy to be here. Neil goes off to visit the bathroom, and Katie and I move over to the side so we don't have to socialize with anyone.

"So things are good with you and Neil?" I ask.

She gives me a funny look. "Whatever. He's someone to get drunk with."

I laugh. "You know, I think you drink more than anyone I know. Even my dad."

"What else is there to do?"

We watch the couples moving around the dance floor. I see Celeste and Jordan, rocking slowly to the music, her head on his shoulder. Close by, Rocco Mackey, in a white tux, is dancing with Dixie Crawford, whose dress shows enough cleavage to start a riot. He sees me looking, flashes a big smile, and grinds his hips into her.

"You should check out the bathrooms in this place," Neil says, coming up beside us. "They're unbelievable."

"Oh no, here we go," Katie says.

"It's a hassle taking a crap when you're wearing a tuxedo, though."

"You see?" Katie says. "This is why I need to drink."

"Come on," Neil says, grabbing her hand. "Let's dance."

"I don't dance," she says.

"Well, maybe we just need to get you another drink," he says. "You coming, Shakespeare?"

I don't want to be left alone, so I follow them back outside. Lisa Kravitz is standing by herself scanning the parking lot. I haven't spoken to her much since that fateful day in Danny Anderson's attic, but I peel away from Neil and Katie now to join her.

"Hi," she says, smiling when she sees me.

She is wearing a strapless red dress and looks amazing. I should tell her. It's what you do on prom night. It wouldn't be like I was hitting on her.

"Hi," I say.

"Have you seen Danny?" she asks.

I look across the lot to where the limos are parked. "Just when I came in. He was headed down there with a few people."

"He's been out here all night," she says.

"You didn't want to go with him?" I remember how much she seemed to enjoy getting high with him two months earlier.

"It's not exactly how I planned to spend my whole evening." She looks around. "Who are you here with?"

"No one, really. Neil and Katie, I guess."

"I thought you were coming with Charlotte," she says.

How does she know this? "I was," I say, "but she couldn't come."

"That's too bad." Lisa looks out at the parking lot once more, then turns to me. "Do you want to go inside and dance?"

Lisa Kravitz is asking me to dance? I don't know how to dance. I'll probably step on her feet.

"Come on," she says, taking my hand.

She leads me inside and onto the dance floor. People glance at us, and I feel a sense of pride having this lovely girl by my side and knowing that people are probably looking at me in a new light. This, I think, is what I always imagined prom to be.

It's a fast song, and I do my best to move to the music without looking ridiculous. I am embarrassed to look Lisa in the eyes, but each time I do, she smiles as if she is genuinely happy to be here dancing with me right now. The song winds down, and I pray that a slow one will come on next. Then I can just sway back and forth and hold Lisa in my arms and feel her body pressed against mine. And if Danny does not come back, if she is feeling lonely and abandoned, maybe she will put her head on my shoulder and who knows what else? The song ends, and a slow song begins. I open my arms in invitation.

"There you are," Danny says, coming up beside us. His eyes are bloodshot, and he reeks of pot. "Hey, Shakespeare." He takes Lisa in his arms and kisses her on the mouth. "Let's dance," he says.

She gives me a guilty look. "Do you mind?"

"No, go ahead," I say, and make my way quickly to the door and back outside. I feel sick to my stomach and know that I can't stay here any longer. I will find Neil and Katie, and if they don't want to leave, I will just have the limo driver take me home. I should never have come in the first place. Why do I always allow myself to be pulled into situations that I know will end badly?

I find our limo. When I open the door, I see Neil and Katie inside, making out. I close the door and wait.

Neil comes out quickly with Katie just behind. "Hey," he says stupidly. "We lost you."

"I'm gonna go," I say.

"What do you mean?" Neil says. "It's only, like, ten o'clock."

"Here, have a drink," Katie says, offering me her flask.

"I don't want a drink."

"Too good to drink with us," she says.

I shake my head. "This night is bad enough already. I don't need to top it off by getting puking drunk."

"The bathrooms are really nice," Neil says.

"I'm really tired," I say. "Can I just borrow the limo to take me home?"

Neil and Katie look at each other. "I guess so," Neil says. "Do you want us to come?"

"No, you guys stay. Really." I climb into the limo and wave. "Call me tomorrow if you're not too hungover."

It is a strange feeling to be sitting in the back of a limousine on prom night, a little bit drunk and utterly alone. What am I doing here? Why am I not at prom like everyone else, celebrating this night in a final burst of teenage revelry and hedonism? Neil and Katie, Celeste and Jordan, Lisa and Danny, even Jane Blumeberg and Eugene Gruber—everybody is with somebody except me.

It strikes me that this would be a perfect image to close my memoir. I have been working on my final chapter and struggling with the ending. What if I were to flash forward a year to the present and try to capture this moment—me, riding home alone in the back of a limousine on prom night while all around the sounds of celebration echo in my ears? A fitting coda to the tragedy of my existence.

I think back to the final days of last summer, just before the start of my senior year. It was a warm August night, and I was sitting on my front steps, thinking about how this year was going to be different, how I was finally going to take charge of my life and get myself a girlfriend and make up for time lost and wasted. What happened to me? How did I end up alone in a limousine on prom night?

I don't want to go home. I don't want to face my parents, who will ask why I am home so early. I don't want to face my brother's empty room and know that on my prom night I am home and he is out with his girlfriend doing things I have never done. Most of all, though, I don't want to face myself and know that once again I just sat back and let life pass me by without even trying to do something about it.

I knock on the glass that separates me from the driver and tell him where I want to go.

It is just after 10:30 when the limousine pulls up in front of Charlotte's housing development. People loitering on the street point and stare, and the driver asks if I'm sure this is where I want to be. I tell him I'll be back soon and climb from the car. I feel nervous walking out in my tuxedo, but my adrenaline is racing and I walk resolutely across the playground to

Charlotte's building and follow a woman inside. I've had a lot of time on the way over to think about what I will say when I see Charlotte, but now as I climb the stairs my head feels strangely blank and I move forward on impulse and instinct.

I stand outside her door and take a deep breath. Inside, I hear the television set playing, but no voices. I lift my hand and knock.

There is shuffling inside, and I hear Henry's voice ring out in challenge. "Who is it?"

"It's Shakespeare," I say. "Charlotte's friend."

I hear Charlotte's voice, and then she opens the door and sees me standing there in my tuxedo, and her eyes open wide in disbelief.

"Hi," I say. "Sorry I'm late."

"W-what are you doing here?" she stammers.

"Tonight's the prom," I say. Noticing Henry and their father on the couch staring at me, I step inside, say hello to Henry, and extend my hand to Charlotte's father, who is slouched over a beer, still in his painter's clothes. "Hello, Mr. White," I say. "I'm Shakespeare."

Charlotte's father shakes my hand and looks quizzically at his daughter. He seems a shadow of the vibrant young man in the framed photograph, and looking at him now, it is easy to see why he has been unable to cobble together a stable life for his children.

"What's with the penguin suit?" Henry says.

"Hey, Henry," I say, "how would you like to go for a ride in a limousine?"

"Shakespeare," Charlotte says.

"I'll go," Henry says, getting up.

"Hold on," Charlotte's father says. "What's all this about?" He does not seem angry, merely confused.

"I'm sorry," I say. "I was supposed to take Charlotte to the prom tonight, but yesterday I did something really stupid and screwed everything up." I pause and turn to Charlotte, who is staring at me, speechless. "I ended up going by myself," I tell her, "but it was horrible to be there alone. I came here to say I'm sorry and to ask if you would still consider coming out with me tonight."

Charlotte does not speak or move even though we are all staring at her. Finally, Henry breaks the silence. "If she says no, do I still get to ride in the limo?"

"Dad," she says, "weren't you going out?"

"Not tonight." He gets up, walks to her, and puts his arm around her shoulder. "Go," he says. "You should go."

She looks at each of us, and Henry nods. "I need a few minutes," she says softly, and goes back into the bedroom and closes the door.

"Is there a TV in the limo?" Henry asks.

I smile. "There sure is."

"Is there a DVD player?"

I nod.

"Are the windows bulletproof?"

"I don't think so," I say.

He looks disgusted. "What kind of cheap limousine doesn't have bulletproof windows?"

"I'm glad you're taking Charlotte out," her father says. "She spends so much time worrying about me and Henry, she never gets a chance to enjoy herself."

I want to tell him that if he did his job as a father, she wouldn't have to worry so much, but when I look at him, he evokes more sympathy than anger.

When the door to the bedroom opens and Charlotte steps out, it takes me a second to register that this is the same girl who left us just moments ago. She is wearing a dress that seems woven together from different fabrics, a little old-fashioned maybe, but somehow exactly right for her.

"Wow," I say. "You look great."

Henry is smiling. "I didn't tell him about the dress."

Charlotte's father seems transfixed, as if he can't believe he is looking at his daughter. There is so much tenderness in his eyes that it is impossible to think he would ever intentionally hurt his children.

"Charlotte made it," Henry says. "I helped her find the fabric."

"You made it?" I say. "When?" And then suddenly it hits me, and the understanding registers on my face.

Charlotte blushes. "I was staying home anyway to try to get caught up on my work. I should have told you. I wanted it to be a surprise."

"Can we go in the limo already?" Henry asks.

"Go," his father says to all of us. "Have fun."

The limousine is parked right where I got out, and the driver is standing outside, smoking a cigarette and talking to a group of teenage boys gathered around.

"Is that your car?" they ask us when we come up.

"What do you think?" Henry says.

We climb in, and I ask Henry where he wants to go.

"I don't care," he says, trying out all the switches and gadgets.

Charlotte leans forward to talk to the driver. "Can you just have us back here in about twenty minutes?"

I feel my heart sink. "Why so soon?"

She motions at Henry. "For him, not me."

Twenty minutes later, we walk Henry back to their building and set off again.

"Aren't you sharing this limousine with Neil and Katie?" Charlotte asks.

"Oh shit," I say. "What time is it?" I look at my watch. "I totally forgot. Prom ends in half an hour. They must be wondering where it is."

"Did you tell them you were taking it?"

"Yeah, but just to go home."

"Home?" She looks at me.

I nod.

"But you came to get me?"

I smile. "I guess I changed course."

When we get to the banquet hall, prom has already begun to empty out. We look around the parking lot and walk inside. Nobody pays us much attention or notices that we have just arrived. I see Lisa and ask her if she has seen Neil or Katie.

"Where did you disappear to?" she says, and then, noticing Charlotte, "Oh, hi."

Charlotte smiles.

"Have you seen them?" I ask.

"I saw Katie throwing up outside about twenty minutes ago. She didn't look so good."

"Let's check the bathrooms," I say.

"If you see Danny," Lisa says, "tell him where I am."

I find Neil standing outside the girls' bathroom. His jacket and bow tie are off, and he has unbuttoned the top two buttons of his shirt.

"Shakespeare!" he yells, falling into me and giving me a hug. "I am so wasted."

"I can see that," I say, untangling myself. "Where's Katie?"

"In there. Throwing up, I think."

"I'll go check on her," Charlotte says, pushing through the bathroom door.

"Where were you?" Neil slurs. "Didn't you leave before?"

"It's a long story. We have the limo outside."

"Did you see the bathrooms? The bathrooms are nice."

"They're very nice," I say. "Let's come over here and sit down." I lead Neil to a chair and sit beside him.

"You're my best friend in the world," Neil says.

I stifle a laugh. "Thanks, Neil. Let's just prop you up a bit."

Charlotte comes out, half supporting Katie beside her. There are stains on Katie's dress, her eyes are like slits, and her face looks green.

We make our way back to the limousine, Charlotte supporting Katie and me supporting Neil.

"I don't want anyone throwing up in my car," the driver says when he sees us.

"Let's just get them home," I say.

Inside the car, I take off my jacket and bow tie and unbutton the top buttons of my shirt. Neil passes out almost immediately after we start moving, and we practically have to carry him inside his house. Katie is slumped in her seat looking thoroughly miserable, and when we pull up to her house, she stumbles from the car and vomits on the sidewalk before pulling herself together and staggering inside.

All this time Charlotte and I have been so focused on Neil and Katie that it comes as a bit of a shock when we find ourselves alone.

"Well," I say. "Here we are." It's strange how nervous I suddenly feel. I've never been nervous with Charlotte before. "What should we do?"

"I should probably go home," she says hesitantly. "I don't want my father to worry."

I start to nod, but then I catch myself. "He won't worry," I say. "He's happy you're out."

"I know," she says, "but it's really late, and I have to help Henry catch up on all his work this weekend, and I still haven't finished my memoir, and—"

I put my hand on her arm. "Charlotte, stop for a minute."

She looks at me, and I see that this moment is as scary for her as it is for me.

"Do you really want to go home now?" I ask.

We are sitting right next to each other, our knees touching, our faces turned together.

"No," she says quietly.

"Where should we go?" My voice is even softer than hers.

Our eyes lock. "Let's go to the beach," she says.

I lean forward and tell the driver, my heart racing, my mind swirling with images culled from romantic movie moments and my own depraved imagination. This night is turning into a fairy tale, I think. Soon we will be making love on soft white sand against a backdrop of breaking waves and moonlit water.

I sit back and take Charlotte's hand in mine. "I'm glad you're staying out," I say.

She smiles. "Me too."

There is no question now that something is going to happen, and the anticipation is intoxicating. Charlotte is looking at me expectantly, and I reach out and stroke her cheek.

"Hi," I whisper.

She leans forward and her mouth brushes gently against mine, moves to my nose, my forehead, then back to my mouth and lingers. We kiss gently at first, then more urgently. I angle my body so I can get at her mouth more easily.

"Wait," she says, pulling away. "You're crushing my leg." She readjusts herself and pulls me back toward her. "That's better."

I thought I had learned something about kissing from Celeste, but the way Charlotte holds each of my lips in hers, the way her tongue runs gently across my teeth and darts in and out of my mouth, I feel myself nearly bursting with desire.

Our hands begin to roam over each other's bodies openly and brazenly. Both of us are breathing heavily, and Charlotte is moaning quietly.

"Hold on," I say. "I'm falling off the seat." I pull myself up and we sit there, catching our breath and laughing.

"Your hair's all messed up," she says, running her hand back and forth across it and messing it up even more.

"Look at your dress," I say, pointing to a tear in the hemline.

She fingers the rip. "Whoever made this thing needs to learn how to sew."

I close my eyes and begin to pat Charlotte all over her body. "Where are you?" I say frantically. "I've gone blind."

"I'm down here," she says, dragging me off the seat. We collapse on the floor, laughing hysterically.

When we get to the beach, we find it overrun. Everywhere we look, there are people drinking beer, making noise, and camping out on blankets. We take off our shoes and walk down to the water. I give Charlotte my jacket because it is so cold. We don't have anything to sit on, so we stand, and my feet become caked with wet sand. Fifty feet away, a group of our classmates is singing very loudly and very off-key.

"This was a good idea, don't you think?" she says.

"It was a great idea. Do you think there are any crabs here?" I try to make it sound like a joke.

She laughs and takes my hand and we look out at the water. I know I should feel something deep or spiritual, and I try to clear my head and let my mind roam free. The waves, I think. Look how the water rushes in and then flows back out. The ocean. There's a whole world underneath the surface. It's so big. As far as the eye can see. I need to pee. Where am I going to pee?

"What are you thinking?" Charlotte asks.

"Nothing, really. It's just nice to look at the water."

"Mom used to love to look at the ocean," she says, as much to herself as to me. "I remember she used to stand on the beach looking out, almost like she was hypnotized. Then she would run straight into the breaking waves and dive under, even though the water was freezing. I think it was the only place she ever felt really happy. It was like everywhere else she felt caged in."

"I remember that picture you showed me," I say.

"It's funny. That's the only picture my dad keeps out, but after my mom died he never wanted to go to the beach anymore. I can't remember the last time I was here."

"Is that why you wanted to come tonight?"

"Maybe," she says. "I don't know. I had forgotten what it feels like to look at the ocean."

I gesture toward the drunken chorus, now belting out a frightening rendition of "We Are the Champions." "What do you think your mom would say if she could see this?"

Charlotte laughs. "I don't know. But I think she would be happy to know I was here."

"Can I ask you something?" I say after a moment.

She turns to me, and her face glows in the moonlight. "Of course."

"Where do you think would be the best place around here to go to the bathroom?"

* * *

The sun is just starting to rise when the limousine pulls up in front of Charlotte's housing development, and all around us the world is sleeping. We walk hand in hand across the deserted playground and stand together in front of the door to her building.

"Well, I guess this is good night," Charlotte says.

I lean over and kiss her and then gently stroke the side of her face. "Good night," I say.

She turns and walks into her building, and after a moment I walk slowly back to the limousine.

Soon I will be home. I will creep up to my room, dump my clothes in a heap, and tumble into a bed that has never felt so welcoming. I will end up sleeping most of the day, and I will not dream anything I can remember. Later, when I wake up, I will call to check on Neil and Katie, I will answer my parents' queries about the night in an infuriatingly vague way, and I will sit down at my computer to finish writing my memoir.

THE TIME I BECAME
A PUBLISHED AUTHOR

I was always in such rebellion against my name that for a long time I was not willing to concede the fact that I might actually be a good writer. I had spent years constructing a narrative for myself in which my name was a major source of my problems, and suddenly to discover that my name might actually signal my one area of strength was not something I was willing to admit.

What could I make, then, of the fact that my highest grades so far in high school were all coming in my English classes? How could I explain the way I rushed to read every edition of the school literary magazine just to see how the published writing stacked up against my own?

By the beginning of eleventh grade, I surrendered. Maybe I was a good writer. My life was still a disaster and the world was still treating me unfairly, but writing was something I could do, and maybe it was time to embrace that gift and see what I could get out of it.

I began to consider submitting some of my writing to the school literary magazine, but I always balked when the signs went up soliciting submissions. I came up with all sorts of explanations for my behavior—my work was too personal, my material inappropriate, my stories too long—but the simple truth was that I could not bear the thought of one more form of rejection in a life weighed down by failure and disappointment. Writing was one thing I thought myself good at, and I had no intention of allowing the editors of the school literary magazine to tell me otherwise.

Our school magazine was called *Red Herring*, a name that struck me as being a little bit clever and very pretentious. In theory, anybody could sign up to be an editor of the magazine, but it was understood that this was an extracurricular activity meant to attract only a certain type—that is, students who dressed mostly in black, drank coffee and smoked cigarettes, spent their free time in the periodical room having discussions with big words, and talked too much in their English classes. In other words, students who struck me as being a little bit clever and very pretentious.

In the spring of junior year, inspired by that memorable drunken conversation in Rome the previous summer, I decided to rewrite the flood story from the Bible. I did not show what I was working on to anyone except Neil, who immediately began pressing me to submit it to the literary magazine.

"I don't know," I said. Neil loved everything I wrote. This did not mean it would be accepted.

"Come on. This is brilliant."

"Those pompous assholes think they're the only ones in the school who can write," I said.

"You know what you should do? Submit this anonymously. It will drive them crazy trying to figure out who the author is."

I shook my head. "I don't know."

"What have you got to lose? If they don't like it, then nobody ever knows it was you.

But if they do, and can't figure out who wrote it, they'll do that thing where they write the letter to you in the next school newspaper asking who you are. Then you can decide if you want to tell them or not."

I thought about this. "Maybe I could submit it under a pseudonym."

"Pseudonym, homonym, whatever. Just submit it."

So, for the first time in my high school career, just two months shy of finishing eleventh grade, I submitted a piece of writing to *Red Herring* and its coffee-drinking, cigarette-smoking, black-turtleneck-wearing, big-word-using board of editors. Neil had made it seem like a no-lose situation, but I knew that if no letter appeared for me in the next issue of the school paper, I would be as devastated as if the paper were to proclaim my failure in a front-page headline.

The paper came out every month, and I had two weeks to wait until the next issue. I knew the editors of *Red Herring* were working to get out their magazine by the middle of May, so if there was no letter for me in the

next issue of the paper, I would know my
piece had not been accepted.

And then two weeks had passed and on page
thirteen of the newspaper there was a short
blurb, one of several short blurbs, and it
said:

We, the editors of *Red Herring*, would
like to include the following
anonymous (and pseudonymous)
submissions in our next issue:
"Soliloquy in Black and White," "My
Dinner with Nero," and "Noah
Revisited." If the authors of these
pieces wish to reveal themselves, we
ask them to do so immediately, and to
consider, also, joining our magazine
as future editors.

I had submitted the piece under the
pseudonym Samuel Clemens, which was Mark
Twain's birth name, and this struck me as
being a little bit clever and very
pretentious. The question now was whether to
stick with my alternate identity or whether
to reveal myself to the magazine's editors.

What everything really boiled down to was whether short-term recognition or long-term mystique was more likely to help me land a girlfriend. With only six weeks left of school, the decision was simple.

I imagined that once the new issue of *Red Herring* appeared, my life would suddenly change. People would admire me. I would overhear conversations about how funny my piece was. Girls would compliment me on my writing. I would be somebody worth knowing.

And I had good reason to think so. The day I found out my piece had been accepted, I revealed myself to Celeste Keller, who was an editor of the magazine, and she told me how funny she thought the piece was and touched my arm. The next day, the editor in chief of *Red Herring,* Jordan Miller, passed me in the hall and asked if I was Shakespeare Shapiro.

"I loved your piece," he said. "It's good for the magazine to get something so different and edgy. Have you ever submitted anything before?"

I told him I had not.

"Well, I hope you'll submit more next

year. And by the way, I love your name."

I walked away with a smile on my face and replayed the conversation in my mind over and over. Jordan Miller. How cool was that? I had always thought he was a pompous asshole, but that was just out of jealousy. Really he was a great guy.

"There's Jordan Miller," I said to Neil the next day. "Let's go over and say hi."

"Why would we do that?"

"He's really cool. Come with me. I don't want to go alone."

Neil gave me a contemptuous look. "What, do you have a crush on him or something?"

I blushed. "Forget it," I said.

When the magazine came out, I turned quickly to my piece and tried to imagine what it would be like to read it for the first time.

Noah Revisited
Prologue
"'So God created man in his own image, in the image of God created he him; male and female created he them.'" God put down the manuscript and gave the

angel in front of him a contemptuous look. "Garbage. Absolute garbage."

"I'm sorry, sir. The humans you commissioned just aren't very good."

"How hard could it be? I asked them to tell the story of the Creation in as much detail as possible. I didn't say tell the story of the Creation using as many pronouns as possible."

The angel blanched. "I think he was just trying to emphasize the importance of the act."

"The only thing he was emphasizing is how much of an idiot he is." God pressed a button on his intercom. "Judy, send in Gabriel." He turned back to the quivering angel. "From now on, I don't even want to see it unless it's publishable."

Gabriel entered and took a seat in front of the Lord. "What's up, Boss?"

"What kind of writing have you been seeing?" God asked.

"Oh, you know, some historical fiction, a few vignettes, a couple of family trees—"

"No, damn it, what's the quality of the writing?"

"Oh. It's pretty weak."

God raised an eyebrow. "Pretty weak?"

"All right, it's awful. Listen to what one human wrote. Let's see, where is it? Enoch . . . Methuselah . . . Lamech . . . ah, here it is. 'And God saw the light, that it was good.' Can you believe it? He's talking about the creation of light, and the best adjective he can come up with is 'good'? *Tremendous, miraculous, divine* . . . but *good?*"

God slammed his almighty hands down on his desk. "I tell them what I want, I tell them how I want it, and those lamebrained good-for-nothing morons still fuck it up. I ought to kill the lot of them."

Chapter 1

And it came to pass that Noah was sitting at his desk proofreading his latest piece of writing.

"Honey, tell me how this sounds. 'And Cain knocked his brother, Abel, silly.'"

"It sounds fine, dear. Now, why don't you stop working for a while? You've been revising that story for days."

"I know, I know. I'm just still not satisfied with it."

"NOAH."

"Not now, honey, I'll lose my train of thought."

"I didn't say anything."

"NOAH."

"Who said that? What do you want?"

"NOAH, IT IS ME. No, no, that's not right . . . NOAH, IT IS I. I hate those damn pronouns."

"Oh, Lord, you scared me. I hate when you speak in capital letters."

"Noah, I need you to build an ark."

"An ark? What's an ark?"

"You think I should call it something else?"

"I don't know. What is it?"

"It's like a boat or a ship."

"I can't build a ship. I'm a writer."

"I don't have time to argue. Either you build yourself a damn ark, or you drown with the rest of mankind."

"Whoa, slow down a second. What do you mean 'drown'?"

"Drown. Under water. What's the matter, you don't understand English?"

"Drown the world? What a great idea for a story."

"You think so?"

"Absolutely. Hold on while I jot this down. Let's see . . . 'flood to destroy mankind.' Great. Now tell me why you're destroying mankind."

"They don't listen to a damn thing I say."

"Well, what did they do?"

"Just listen to this writing. 'And Adam knew Eve, his wife.' Of course he knew her. They were the only two people on the planet. Why doesn't he just say what he means, that he fu—"

"You're drowning them because they can't write? I don't buy it. Give me something more believable. Drugs, prostitution, incest. There must be some of that."

"Well, of course there's incest. When you start off with only one family in the world, your little sister starts to look pretty good."

"Well, maybe I'll just say there was some kind of general wrongdoing. Anyway, instead of building an ark, let me shape this into a draft."

"I don't know . . ."

"One night, that's all I need."

"Okay. But you still have to build the ark when you finish . . . Oh, and Noah . . . don't call me 'The Big Cheese' in this one. 'God' or 'The Lord' will do just fine."

Chapter 2

And it came to pass that God was reading the story that Noah had submitted.

"FORTY DAYS? ARE YOU OUT OF YOUR
MIND? NOBODY WILL BELIEVE THAT IT
RAINED FOR FORTY DAYS."

"Well, twenty days certainly isn't
enough to drown the world. Haven't you
ever heard of the willing suspension
of disbelief? If you can have
characters living nine hundred years,
you can certainly have a flood that
lasts forty days."

"And look at this. 'Too of every
animal went into the ark.'"

"What's the matter with that?"

"*TWO*. T-W-O. T-O-O MEANS 'ALSO.'"

"Anything else?"

"Yeah. The snake's not going."

Chapter 3

And it came to pass that Noah
constructed an ark and prepared to set
sail.

"Aardvarks?"

"Here."

"Aardwolves?"

"Here."

"Abyssinian cats?"

"Here."

"Addaxes?"

"Here."

"Adders?"

"Here."

"Adélie penguins?"

"Here."

Chapter 4

And it came to pass that Noah kept a
diary during his voyage:

CAPTAIN'S LOG, DAY 1: After three days
of calling roll, we finally set sail.
We all stood on the deck and waved
good-bye to our friends who had come
to see us off. The poor, unsuspecting
fools.

My wife has been against this ark
since I first mentioned it. For the
past three days, it's been nag, nag,
nag. "Since when did you become a
sailor?" Or, "Since the kids were
born, you've refused to get them a

pet, and now all of a sudden you're an
animal lover?" It took me hours of
begging just to get her on the ark,
and then she went straight to her room
and locked the door.

CAPTAIN'S LOG, DAY 2: It looks like I
didn't give enough thought to my
rooming assignments. At breakfast this
morning a bunch of animals said they
had already eaten. That was when I
discovered that about one hundred
species had become extinct.

As for my own rooming, my wife
refused to let me in, but I spent a
surprisingly satisfying night with the
sheep.

CAPTAIN'S LOG, DAY 5: The sheep kicked
me out last night when I suggested we
invite the goats over for a little
threesome. Word must have gotten
around that I was some kind of
pervert, because none of the other
animals would let me in. Despair.

CAPTAIN'S LOG, DAY 10: I have been
feverishly writing love poems to my
wife in an effort to win her back.

Beloved wife, I miss you much,
Your tender and caressing touch.
With other women I may dabble,
But only you raise me up like the
Tower of Babel.

CAPTAIN'S LOG, DAY 11:
There once was a man who was sore
'Cuz his wife wouldn't open the
door.
Celibacy
Is just not for me
Let me in, you cock-teasing whore.

CAPTAIN'S LOG, DAY 17: The animals are
getting restless, and there is talk of
mutiny. This morning, one of the
lions came to me with a list of
demands. (I wonder who died and made
him king.) In particular, there seems
to be mounting displeasure with my
9:00 curfew.

My wife is still not speaking to
me, and masturbation has proven a poor
substitute.

CAPTAIN'S LOG, DAY 36: We spotted the
white whale today and gave chase. The
creature reared its mighty head and
spurted a towering stream of water
into the air. I found this strangely
arousing.

Chapter 5

And it came to pass after forty days
and forty nights that God remembered
his covenant with Noah.

"So we agreed we'd split the
profits 70-30, right?" God said.

"You said 50-50."

"That was before I got ahold of
this juicy little diary of yours.
Let's see . . . Captain's Log, Day 29.
I'm so horny I could—"

"All right, all right, 70-30. Just
don't show it to my wife. Besides,
it's not like there's anybody alive

to buy this damn flood story anyway."

"Patience, Noah, patience. Thousands of years from now, it's going to be a bestseller."

"That's easy for you to say. I've only got a few hundred years left."

Epilogue

"'And ye shall circumcise the flesh of your foreskins . . . And the uncircumcised man-child whose flesh of his foreskin is not circumcised, that soul shall be cut off from his people.'" God put down the manuscript and gave the angel in front of him a contemptuous look. "Disgusting. Absolutely disgusting."

"I'm sorry, sir. I thought you wanted me to tell the writers to add more gratuitous violence."

"Yes, but I didn't mean messing with people's genitals."

The angel blanched. "I think he was just trying to emphasize the importance of the covenant."

"The only thing he was emphasizing

is how much of a pervert he is." God
pressed a button on his intercom.
"Judy, send in Abraham." He turned
back to the quivering angel. "Tell the
humans to be careful what they wish
for."

Abraham entered and took a seat in
front of the Lord. "What's up, Boss?"

God sighed. "I need your advice
about these Sodomites."

That day, a few people I knew told me
they liked my piece, but nobody showed half
the enthusiasm of Neil, who carried his
magazine around all day and told everybody
he saw to read my story and that he was best
friends with the author.

At the end of the day, my brother, who
was a freshman, came up to me with a group
of his friends.

"This is my brother," he said to them.

"I liked your piece in the literary
magazine," one of the kids said.

"Thanks."

This was nice. Gandhi, who usually
ignored me in school, was now bragging about

me to his friends. At least I had some kind of fan club, even if they were ninth graders.

"Hey, Shakespeare, can you tell Mom I had to stay late at school to work on a project, and I'll be home by dinner?"

"Okay. What are you working on?"

He smiled. "Science. You know, the effects of certain substances on the human brain?"

My brother's friends started to laugh.

"I don't remember studying that."

"Too bad," he said, starting to walk away. "It's really fascinating. Tell Mom I'll be home by dinner."

I watched them strut down the hall laughing. Great. My brother, who was a freshman, already had a richer social life than I did. What was going on? I was a published author. Where were all my friends? Where was everybody who wanted to hang out after school with me? Where were the girls? Where was the recognition?

One day passed and then another. People had read their copies of *Red Herring* and left them lying around the school. The year was winding down, students were talking about plans for the summer, seniors were gearing up for prom and graduation, and everyone, it seemed, was hooking up with everyone else. My brother appeared in the hallway one day holding hands with a girl from his class. Celeste Keller began showing up mornings in Jordan Miller's car and driving off with him each day when school let out. All around me, people were moving on, growing up, probably having sex, and here I was, still watching from the sidelines, seventeen years down and nothing to show for it.

School ends. I spend the summer at home working as a camp counselor, watching potential girlfriends get picked off one by one by boys less timid, and waiting for something to happen, which of course never does. It's okay, I convince myself. Soon school will start again, and I will have the whole of senior year stretched out in front of me and everything will be different. I have already begun to make a name for myself by being published in the literary magazine,

but it was too little too late. This year I
will step firmly into the limelight,
establish myself as a daring and original
writer, and become somebody people actually
talk about. My senior memoir will be my
canvas. By exploiting the tragedy of my
life, by brazenly documenting the most
cringe-inducing episodes of a cringe-filled
existence, I will achieve a kind of cult-
hero status. I sit on my steps on a warm
August night, close my eyes, and imagine the
possibilities.

JUNE

Dear Shakespeare,

    Congratulations on being picked as a memoir finalist. Didn't I always tell you how good a writer you are? This year has been so unpredictable and tumultuous, but I really value the time we spent together. Sometimes I wish I could be more like you, the way you have a sense of humor about everything and don't always take yourself so seriously. I think we were good for each other——I just hope I didn't drive you too crazy. You're probably writing something incredibly witty in my yearbook right now, and here I am, babbling on. Jordan and I are going to Europe in July, but I'll be around in August if you want to get together for a cup of coffee or a movie.

    Fondly,

      Celeste

Dear Celeste,

    Good luck at Brown next year. Maybe I'd be there with you, except they told me I wasn't good enough. They actually wait-listed me at first and made me believe I had a real chance of getting in, but that was just a tease until they got a firm commitment from people they were always more interested in. (Sorry about that, I couldn't resist.) I really am happy we became so close this year, and even though you tormented me, I know it was not done intentionally or out of malice. In the end, I am grateful to you for appreciating who I am and seeing things in me that I was too insecure to recognize in myself.

        Adiós,

        Shakespeare

Dear Shakespeare,

    You would not believe the crap I took this morning. It was one of those craps that just keeps coming and coming in waves, and you keep thinking you're done, and then you feel another wave coming on. It was probably one

of the ten best shits I've taken this year.
Hey, can you believe we're graduating? We've
done so much together these past four
years—getting drunk for the first time,
going to the sex doctor, staying up all night
watching bad movies on TV, talking on our
cell phones while we were taking craps.
I actually wrote about that in my memoir, you
know? Anyway, you're the writer, not me, so
I'm signing off.

Your partner in crime,
Neil

Dear Neil,
  It's hard to believe that I'm such good
friends with someone who spends all his
time either shitting or talking about
shitting. It's even harder to believe that
Katie went out with you this year. I guess
it was inevitable that it wouldn't last, what
with Katie moving out west and you being
the tremendous freak that you are. Oh well.
You're going to college now anyway. Time
to flush the toilet and start with a fresh
bowl. What more can I say? You're a

great friend, and without you these past
four years would have been even shittier
than they were.

      With all due respect, admiration,
      and concern for your well-being,
      Shakespeare

Shakespeare,
    I hate all this yearbook-signing bullshit. What
the hell do you want me to say? I'm not going to
miss this place, I don't want to hold on to any
memories, and I'm probably never going to see
you again after I graduate. All right, maybe I'll
see you, but only if you're still together with
Charlotte. At least you did something right
before you graduated.

      Later,
      Katie

Dear Katie,
    We should go out after graduation and
get drunk. Just kidding. I really do respect
the fact that you've given up drinking since
prom, even if it has made you more

foulmouthed and ornery than ever. I'm glad
you and Charlotte became friends. It's nice
that the two women in my life get along
with each other so well. By the way,
I think Charlotte's brother has a crush on
you. Oh yeah, I almost forgot. Have fun
with Rocco at college.
>   Cheers,
>   Shakespeare

SHAKESPEARE,
    I HOPE YOU'RE WRITING SOME FUNNY SHIT
IN MY YEARBOOK. I WISH I COULD WRITE LIKE
YOU. YOU'VE GOT A SICK MIND, BRO.
    HEY, CHECK THIS OUT.
    IT'S A DRAWING OF MR. PARKE'S
LEFT TESTICLE.
>   YOU'RE THE MAN.
>   ROCCO

Dear Rocco,
    Explain something to me. How is it that
someone who refers to girls in class as chicks,
laughs every time he hears the name Dick,
includes violent drawings with the work he
turns in, talks incessantly about how much

he can bench-press, and thinks <u>Dude,</u>
<u>Where's My Car?</u> is the greatest movie ever
made is able to get laid on such a consistent
basis? Good luck in college. I'd stay away
from Katie if I were you.
                    Shakespeare

Dear Shakespeare,
    It was cool getting to know you this year. I wish
we could have had even more <u>high</u> times.
Remember that time you came over? Dude, you
were so wasted. After graduation, we should
celebrate big-time. Be cool. Stay sane. Have a nice
life.
              You're a good man, Charlie Brown.
              Danny

Dear Danny,
    Read this only after you have taken
many, many bong hits.
    the floor is on the ceiling where the
lightning slides abound in the river of the
spinning tulips marching all around where
the wheels turn in the doorknobs and
banana marching bands float through the

cloudy rainbow streams of heavy breathing
sands endless chanting endless chanting
endless chanting endless chanting endless
chanting endless chanting endless chanting
bend less panting the sky is your mother
I am the walrus.
Milkshakespeare
Shakespearmint

Dear Shakespeare,

The scariest thing for me is thinking about
how I almost closed you out of my life. This has
not been an easy year. I learned a long time
ago to deal with my brother's issues and my
father's, but it was much harder for me to begin
to address my own. Thank you for not giving up
on me. Thank you for being able to see that I
needed help even though I put up so many walls
to prevent anyone from helping me. If it weren't
for you and Mr. Basset, I probably wouldn't be
graduating on time. There's so much more I want
to say, but I'm afraid if Katie reads this, it
might drive her back to drinking. Besides, we
have the whole summer to talk.
Love,
Charlotte

DEAR ABBY,
  I JUST STARTED GOING OUT WITH
THIS GIRL AND I REALLY LIKE HER A LOT.
I WANT TO WRITE SOMETHING TO HER
THAT WILL EXPRESS HOW I FEEL, BUT
EVERYTHING I THINK OF SOUNDS LIKE A
HALLMARK CARD. WHAT SHOULD I DO?
            SIGNED,
              NEUROTIC

Dear Neurotic,
  I have no fucking idea.

    If Mr. Parke saw this, he would say I'm
trying to use humor to avoid expressing my
true feelings. Trust me. These are my true
feelings. And besides, this isn't even very
humorous. Okay, all kidding aside, I'm
going to be serious now. Take a deep
breath, Shakespeare. Ready? Here goes. On
the count of three. One. Two. Three.
Charlotte . . . (dramatic pause) No, forget
the dramatic pause; that's just using humor
again as a cover. See, I love that I can joke
around with you like this. I love how

comfortable you make me feel with who I
am. To have a girlfriend who also feels like
a best friend is the most wonderful thing I
can imagine, and these past two weeks have
been the happiest time I can remember.
(Cue the sappy music.) I hope you win the
memoir award. What a turn-on it would be
to be dating an award-winning author.
                    Love,
                        Shakespeare

On the day of graduation, we march in alphabetical order and take our seats in the converted gymnasium where the ceremony is being held. I'm between Mudit Shah, who is off to MIT to study physics, and Rich Sharp, who is off to Penn State to join a fraternity and sexually harass drunken sorority girls.

Our principal welcomes everybody and tells us that he hopes Hemingway High has encouraged us to approach the world with an open mind, to avoid getting boxed in by traditional notions of success, and to experiment freely with our interests and ambitions. Our class valedictorian tells us that Hemingway High has prepared her for her pre-med studies at Harvard and has taught her the importance of setting a course in life and never wavering. Our guest speaker tells us that we are entering a world filled with contradictions.

All three speeches are incredibly boring.

When the time comes to hand out the award for best senior memoir, three people I don't recognize introduce themselves as Hemingway High graduates and previous recipients of the award. They blabber on a bit about writing and writers, and the weird-looking one makes a joke about how when he wrote his memoir, it was the only time in his life when he was actually grateful to have such a dysfunctional family.

Then they get serious, and the woman says, "Before we announce the winner of this year's memoir award, we would like to recognize all of this year's finalists. Please hold your applause until all the names have been read. Madongo Abraham, for his memoir, *Exodus*." Applause. "Cordelia Blythe, for her memoir, *This Girl's Life*." Applause. "If you could please hold your applause until the end," the woman says. "Melissa Brookstream, for her memoir, *Inked Fragments*." A smattering of claps. "Enzo Casablanca, for his memoir, *The Good, the Bad, and My Childhood*." Light laughter. "Avery Cooke, for his memoir, *Stirred, Not Shaken*. Max Gatz, for his memoir, *Portrait of a Jewboy as a Young Man*."

"We love you, Max!" someone screams, and everybody laughs.

"Sally Hill, for her memoir, *Everything I Need to Know I Learned in Kindergarten*. Tristan Potter, for his memoir, *Diary of a Glutton*. Shakespeare Shapiro, for his memoir, *17 Down*. Padma Vajpayee, for her memoir, *Upanishad Is Not a Dirty*

Word. Galaxy Veeder, for her memoir, *Black Holes.* Charlotte White, for her memoir, *Cages.*"

The woman waits for the applause to stop. She turns to her fellow judges and says, "May I have the envelope, please?" and the two men start checking all their pockets and then pretend to panic, before one of them finally comes up with the requested item hidden inside his shoe.

Everybody laughs at this bit of theatrics, and my stomach clenches up in a knot. Oh my God, this is it, I think. I realize how much I want Charlotte to win, or if not her, someone else other than me. It's not so much that I'm afraid of tripping on my way up to the podium, though that is a legitimate concern. It's more the feeling that my winning would somehow change things between us. I know this is my issue, not hers, but it just seems that her memoir is so much more consequential than mine, and that my winning would be an insult to her life and her experiences. Charlotte would hate me for saying this, but I can't help feeling that she deserves this for everything she has gone through and for being brave enough to write about it.

"This year's winner is . . ."

The dramatic pause. I hate the dramatic pause. Get it over with, already.

"Melissa Brookstream, for her memoir, *Inked Fragments.*"

Thunderous applause as Melissa (4.0 GPA, perfect SATs, editor of *Red Herring,* drama club, Yale, cancer survivor) climbs to the stage and accepts her award. I clap politely, a little disappointed that Charlotte has not won, but knowing deep down that she is probably relieved not to have to step into the limelight.

The graduation ceremony winds down, we get our diplomas, throw our caps in the air, pose for pictures with family and friends, shake hands with classmates we barely know, and go off, all of us, with our own entourages to mark the occasion in our own special ways.

My parents have made reservations at a fancy restaurant, and my dad immediately orders a bottle of wine and tells the waitress to bring glasses for all of us. "My son just graduated high school," he says, as if this is justification enough to violate the legal drinking age.

"I can't believe it," my mother says. "How can I possibly be old enough to have a son who's already off to college?"

"Don't get rid of me yet. I still have the summer."

"I wish I was leaving," Gandhi says.

My parents are in high spirits and keep telling me how proud they are. They are dying to read my memoir, but I put them off and tell them that someday, someday I'll let them read it, though it's hard to imagine a scenario in which this will ever happen.

My father raises his wineglass. "To Shakespeare," he says.

"To Shakespeare," my mother and brother repeat.

We clink our glasses and drink.

By the time we order dessert, we have nearly finished a second bottle of wine, and my parents have launched into stories about our childhoods that we have heard a thousand times. Normally, I would have little patience for this, but today I am genuinely enjoying myself. As I sit back and sip my wine, I notice that Jody Simons and Paige Blanchard have just walked into the restaurant with their families in tow. Because I have a girlfriend now, I do not feel the extreme awkwardness and discomfort I would always experience in the presence of girls I fantasized about, nor do I feel the familiar jolt of panic when Jody sees me, waves, and walks over to our table.

"Hi," she says cheerily.

My parents look at her, then look at me, and both begin to smile.

"Hi," I say. "Mom, Dad, this is Jody. She graduated today, also."

"Congratulations," my parents say.

"Thanks. I just wanted to meet you and tell you that Shakespeare is, like, the best name ever."

"You hear that?" my dad says, looking at me. He turns to Jody. "You have no idea how much he's complained about his name."

I smile and shrug, happy to concede this little victory to my parents. I have just graduated. I have a girlfriend. I am sitting in a fancy restaurant sipping wine. Jody Simons has come over to my table of her own free will. I realize that I am feeling completely relaxed and at ease.

"Did we ever tell you how we came up with your name?" my mother asks.

"Yes, Mom," I say, blushing, no longer relaxed, no longer at ease.

Paige walks over to the table and introduces herself to my parents. The situation is becoming hazardous.

"I never heard the story," my brother says, trying hard to keep a straight face. He turns to Paige. "My mother was about to tell us how they came up with Shakespeare's name."

My father takes out his handkerchief and blows a mighty blow.

My mother turns to the girls. "We both loved to act when we were younger, and . . ." She smiles and shakes her head. "I can't believe I'm telling this."

Me neither. Please stop.

She takes a sip of wine. "Well, you have to understand we were a little wild in our younger days."

Tell me this is not happening.

My father puts his arm around me. "Probably not as wild as this one, though."

My brother nods. "Yeah, Shakespeare's a real wild man."

My mother looks at me affectionately. "Isn't he handsome?" she says to the girls.

"Like a stallion," my father says.

"You know," my mother says, "he never tells us anything about his social life."

My father squeezes me harder. "Like a stallion," he bellows. "Just raring to go."

ACKNOWLEDGMENTS

I'd like to thank the following people: my agent, Marcia Wernick, for believing in me as a writer; my editor, Jim Thomas, for providing such thoughtful feedback on the manuscript; and my wife, Kira, for all her love and support.

ABOUT THE AUTHOR

Jake Wizner's life improved significantly after he graduated from high school. These days he lives in New York City with his wife and two daughters and teaches eighth-grade English and history. *Spanking Shakespeare* is his first novel.